The MAGNIFICENT LIZZIE BROWN

and the Fairy Child

Books in
THE
MAGNIFICENT LIZZIE BROWN
SERIES

The
MAGNIFICENT
LIZZIE BROWN
and the
Fairy Child

VICKI LOCKWOOD

Curious Fox CF

6056957

First published in 2015 by Curious Fox,
an imprint of Capstone Global Library Limited,
7 Pilgrim Street, London, EC4V 6LB
Registered company number: 6695582

www.curious-fox.com

Text © Hothouse Fiction Ltd 2015

Series created by Hothouse Fiction
www.hothousefiction.com

The author's moral rights are hereby asserted.

Cover illustration © Eva Morales 2015
Designed by Steve Mead

ISBN 978 1 78202 067 7

19 18 17 16 15
10 9 8 7 6 5 4 3 2 1

A CIP catalogue for this book is available from the British Library.

Typeset in Adobe Garamond Pro by Hothouse Fiction Ltd

Printed and bound by CPI Group (UK) Ltd, Croydon, CRO 4YY

MIX
Paper from
responsible sources
FSC
www.fsc.org   FSC® C020471

With special thanks to
Adrian Bott

CHAPTER 1

Malachy Fitzgerald leaned on his walking stick and stared at Lizzie Brown in disbelief.

'You mean to say you've never heard of King Arthur?'

'I've heard of Queen Victoria,' Lizzie said with a shrug. 'She's the one we've got, and that'll do for me.'

The two children were halfway up the path that threaded up the side of the spectacular mountain called Arthur's Seat. Overlooking the city of Edinburgh, it humped against the skyline like a sleeping dragon.

Lizzie looked down the way they'd come. She could still make out the red and white shape that was the show tent of Fitzy's Travelling Circus, standing out among the green of Holyrood Park. The caravans, including her own, were huddled in a cosy group behind it, as if to keep the chill October winds at bay. Her nose tingled from the sharp, cold air.

It had been a long journey to reach the Scottish city, and after spending hours jolting along in the back of a caravan, the circus folk wanted nothing more than to shoot off and explore the new site. But the work of setting up always came first.

Fitzy, the owner and ringmaster, had a kind heart but wouldn't tolerate slackers. 'A circus is like a pyramid of elephants,' he had told Lizzie once. 'We all stand on one another's shoulders. It only takes one person to slack off, and next thing you know, it's raining elephants.'

So the pegs had been hammered, the boxes unpacked, the animals corralled and the huge tent poles hauled into place, until the circus stood proud and ready. After that, the men were free to go and explore the pubs, while the women headed to the shops and the children did whatever they liked, so long as they stayed out of trouble.

Lizzie, the circus fortune-teller, and Malachy, the owner's son, were remarkably *bad* at staying out of trouble. When Fitzy demanded to know where they were off to, Malachy had told him: 'We're going to climb to the top of Arthur's Seat, Pop.'

'Any particular reason?'

'Best view of the city from up there.'

Fitzy had raised an eyebrow. 'All right. But make sure you're back here by three – I don't want to have to send out a search party because you two were off hunting the wild haggis or some such foolery.'

As they climbed up the mountain, it dawned on Lizzie that Malachy had another reason for wanting to reach the peak. The boy had a club foot, and though he used a walking stick sometimes, he refused to let his disability slow him down. He sometimes set himself physical challenges and forced himself to achieve them. Like this hike.

Halfway up, Lizzie had asked who Arthur was.

Malachy shook his head. 'I can't believe you've never heard of him. He was the legendary King of Britain, back in the olden days. Had a round table all the knights used to sit around … Don't yawn, Liz, it's rude.'

'Don't sound like my sort of story, to be honest.'

'No? There's a witch in it. Bit like you!'

Lizzie laughed and shoved him playfully. 'Tell me about her, then.'

'Ooh, she was evil. Morgan le Fay, her name was. She tried to bring down the kingdom with her wicked schemes. She managed it, in the end, sort of. That's why there's only ruins now.'

'What sort of a name is Morgan le Fay? Sounds French.'

'You're not wrong!' Malachy sounded impressed. 'It means Morgan the Fairy. I bet you thought fairies were just pretty little things, didn't you? Well, they aren't all like that. There's all sorts – dark ones as well as light. Ask Ma Sullivan ... why are you looking at me like that?'

'Because you're totally off your head, sunshine,' Lizzie scoffed, shaking her head. 'Bloomin' fairies. There's no such ruddy thing!'

'It's only a story. You don't have to blow your top over it.' Malachy strode past her without looking back.

She could tell he was struggling, but she knew better than to offer to help him. Now she felt bad for hurting his feelings. 'Sorry, mate. It's just ... there weren't no time for fairy stories back in Rat's Castle where I grew up.'

Rat's Castle was a sprawling London slum of narrow, filthy streets. Some families lived ten to a room, with nothing but a bucket for a bathroom if you were lucky, and no food except for what you could beg or steal. Lizzie thought any fairy that set foot there would shrivel up and die – if fairies had even been real, which of course they weren't.

Even when her mother had been alive, she had never told Lizzie fairy stories. Lizzie wondered why. Maybe she hadn't wanted to fill her daughter's head with the sweet lie of everything ending happily ever after. She had sung, though – old folk songs and street ballads. Those, Lizzie would always remember.

Her father's only stories had been about the drunken fights he'd got into. If he'd won, there would be boasts about how the man he'd beaten up was twice his size, but he'd flattened him with a single punch. If he'd lost, he'd spit out a bitter story about the other man's cheating or the treachery of his friends.

'I don't need fairy tales,' she told Malachy happily. 'Real life's magical enough for me, since I joined up with you lot.'

Fitzy's Circus had blown into Lizzie's life like a glittering tornado, whisking her up and out of the misery of the slums. Now she made her living as the circus's fortune-teller in residence, among larger-than-life characters more strange and wonderful than she could ever have dreamed.

In a way, she herself had become stranger and more wonderful than any of them. Because Lizzie had a power she didn't fully understand. All through her life she had glimpsed the future in her dreams, but it was only when she joined the circus that she learned how to use her clairvoyance to the full.

She was no sideshow fake, but a genuine psychic: the only one in the country, for all she knew. Just by touching someone's palm, she could see into their past and future. She could also speak to the spirits of the dead. Sometimes, visions would strike her without warning, as if some higher power was pointing her towards a wrong that needed to be set right.

She and Malachy walked on. He chatted about King Arthur's legend, while Lizzie admired the view. The mountain was bare, with only a few bushes and patches of scrub, but the sight of the wide open space still thrilled her – she was out of Rat's Castle's stinking streets for good.

'Come on, Lizzie,' Malachy said, wincing. 'We're nearly there.' He strode on ahead of her.

'It's not a bloomin' race!' she shouted.

The mountain's summit was a pitted crown of exposed rock. Malachy went to stand by the edge, shaking his walking stick in triumph, and for a second Lizzie thought he looked like a chieftain from the olden days, brandishing his spear at the city below.

She joined him and sat down on the rough rocks. The view really was as magnificent as they'd been told. Edinburgh was spread out far below them like a map brought to life. Lizzie imagined flying through the clouds like a witch, looking down on the beautiful labyrinth of streets and houses. There was the castle with its battlements and towers, brooding above the rooftops, somehow majestic and haunted at the same time.

'I'm glad we came here,' she said softly. 'I never dreamed I'd travel to a different country.'

'Scotland is beautiful,' Malachy agreed.

Lizzie let her gaze rove over the cityscape, following it round – and then she saw some factories in the distance by the harbour. Like an ugly scab on a child's face, they blighted the whole city. Tall brickwork chimneys stained with soot spewed out black smoke into the sky.

'I don't like them buildings, though,' she said with a shudder. 'They're like monsters. Devils, even. Chewing up everything around them, and belching out poison.'

Malachy laughed out loud. 'Listen to you! You sound like one of those reformists, handing out tracts in the street. "Improve working conditions! People before profits!"'

'But they're horrible! Look at them.'

Malachy stood and hooked his thumbs through his braces. 'That's progress, Liz. It doesn't always look pretty, but it's the future.'

Lizzie turned away. 'It ain't a future I want any part of.'

'Don't be soft,' Malachy said with scorn. 'Industry's a *good* thing. It's what makes this country strong. Rule Britannia and all that.'

'It stinks if you ask me,' said Lizzie, wrinkling her nose in disgust.

The two of them dragged themselves back to the circus camp, arriving worn-out and breathless with three minutes left to go. While Malachy went to help Fitzy prepare for opening night, Lizzie slipped into the show tent to watch the performers rehearse.

A little thrill of satisfaction went through her as she saw she hadn't missed the Astonishing Boissets. They were trapeze artists and high wire walkers – and young

Dru Boisset, at fourteen, was a rising star of the show.

Lizzie watched him walk from one end of the wire to the other with his sister Collette poised on his shoulders. 'Smile!' yelled their father, Pierre. 'I do not care 'ow much it 'urts. Always smile for the crowd.'

Dru smiled and waved to the empty seats. His eye caught Lizzie's, and his smile broadened, becoming real. Lizzie blushed and waved back, her thoughts suddenly in a muddle. Dru seemed to have a lot more muscles than he used to...

Without warning, Collette's smile faltered and became a grimace of pain. Dru seemed to sense something was wrong and hurried to the end of the rope. His sister climbed down the ladder, clutching her back and moving stiffly as a broken doll.

Better give them some privacy, Lizzie thought as the Boissets huddled together to talk. *Something's wrong, by the look of it.*

She went and found her friend Hari in the animal enclosure. Her eyes widened as she saw a furry little creature hopping about in front of Hari. 'Wait, is that a monkey?'

Hari flipped a raisin into the air. The monkey flung itself up, caught the raisin and began to nibble it. 'Lizzie, meet Hanu,' Hari said. 'He's the newest member of our circus menagerie.'

'Hanu?'

'Short for Hanuman – he's one of our Hindu gods. The monkey god.'

Lizzie knelt down for a better look. 'Can I touch him?'

'Of course you can. He's tame.'

Very gently Lizzie reached out and stroked the soft fur on the monkey's head. Hanu glanced up at her with beady black eyes. 'He looks like a little wise old man,' she said, enthralled. Then she jerked back in surprise as Hanu skittered closer. She locked eyes with Hari and kept very still.

The monkey tugged at the fabric of her skirt, then lifted himself up and settled in a warm heap in her lap. He blinked at Lizzie as if to say, 'I can sit wherever I like'.

'I love him,' Lizzie said. 'Wherever did you find a monkey up in Scotland?'

'He was a present from the Maharaja Gurinder Bhatti. To say thank you for the show we put on, and … for the other stuff.'

Lizzie knew exactly what 'the other stuff' was. The

Maharaja had summoned the circus to Whitby, in the north of England, to put on a show for the locals at his expense. But unbeknownst to him, someone close to him had been plotting to steal his prized ruby, the Heart of Durga. It had all been connected to the appearance of a mysterious ghost ship in Whitby Harbour.

The monkey bared his teeth and made a chittering noise. 'He wants to be fed,' Hari explained. 'He always wants food. Greedy little beggar. Here, you feed him.'

He passed Lizzie a date, and she held it gingerly and watched Hanu reach up to take it. They monkey bit, chewed, glanced around as if fearful some other animal would snatch his date away, and then bit again.

'Look at his little fingers,' Lizzie breathed. 'They're just like a person's.' Watching the monkey eat, she realized that she was starving too. She lifted Hanu out of her lap and set him on Hari's shoulder. 'You'd best stay here, little fella. If Ma Sullivan catches you in her tea tent, she'll scream blue murder.'

Ducking into the tea tent, Lizzie saw that her friends Erin and Nora, the Amazing Sullivan Twins, were having their dinner too. Their mother was outside, fetching more wood for the cooking stove.

'Did you make it all the way to the top of Arthur's

Seat?' Erin asked. 'Did Malachy?'

'Course we did,' said Lizzie with her mouth full. 'You can see all the way over the city. Come next time!'

'We can't,' Erin said, kicking the folding table leg. 'Ma won't let us.'

'"Climbing up a mountain? Are yeh mad? What if you twist an ankle, eh?"' said Nora, imitating their mother's Irish brogue.

'"What about your practice? We're not here for a holiday!"' Erin joined in.

'"When you break both your legs, don't come running to me!"' the twin bareback riders finished together, and burst out laughing.

'My ears are burning,' Ma Sullivan said darkly, as she came back into the tea tent. Erin and Nora instantly clammed up. But their eyes still twinkled with silent laughter.

Ma Sullivan had a saucer in her hand, and as Lizzie watched, she added little pieces of food to it. Then she turned to leave.

'Have we got another new animal?' Lizzie frowned. 'I haven't seen a cat around.'

'It's for the Good Folk,' Ma Sullivan said.

Lizzie looked blank.

'She means the fairies,' Nora explained.

Lizzie laughed, not sure if Nora was joking. 'Not you lot as well as Malachy! Am I the only person in the circus who doesn't believe in fairies?'

'Hush, now,' Ma Sullivan said sternly. 'There's more fairies in Scotland than anywhere else in these lands. If you look with your heart, and not just your eyes, you might be lucky enough to see one.'

Nora and Erin nodded. 'You'd best be careful, Liz,' Erin said. 'You've got to treat them right, the fairies. If you don't, they're liable to take it personal.'

'And that,' Nora said with a serious look, 'always means trouble.'

CHAPTER 2

'Right, you bunch of tearaways,' said Fitzy with a grin. 'You all know the routine. Now that the tent's up, we need to rustle up some business. Can't have a circus without punters, can we?'

The Penny Gaff Gang – Lizzie, Dru, Hari, Malachy, Erin and Nora – all knew what was being asked of them. Fitzy had laid out piles of freshly printed posters, leaflets and tickets.

'Promotion!' he announced, putting his thumbs through his braces, just like his son. 'Comes before performance. Not in the dictionary, mind you. Ah, Collette! Nice of you to join us.'

Dru's sister joined them, looking dazzling in a white satin dress bedecked with sequins. As they all gathered up armfuls of posters, Lizzie nudged Dru. 'Ain't she meant to be in rehearsal?'

'Papa excused her from practice because of her bad back,' Dru whispered, 'but you know how Fitzy is. If you can't do one job, he'll find you another.'

'Well, what are you all waiting for?' cried Fitzy. 'Go and get some bums on seats!'

Chatting excitedly, the group of friends headed down into the streets of Edinburgh. Lizzie loved this part of circus life – she could explore a new city, make money for the circus and make the locals' eyes light up with joy all at the same time.

Fitzy's parting shout rang in their ears: 'And try not to wind up the rozzers, for heaven's sake…'

'Us, get into trouble with the police?' Malachy said once his father was out of earshot. 'Whatever gives him that idea?'

Putting up posters for the circus was a street crime, except there wasn't a victim. Two of the children kept lookout, while a third hastily slapped a poster on the wall and slathered it with paste. Then they bustled away, quick as could be, before any patrolling police officers could catch them.

That method worked just fine on the outskirts of the city, where posters could be stuck up on the walls of old buildings, billboards, closed-down shops and abandoned houses, or even nailed to trees. But in the city's heart, where shoppers jostled against one another, they had to use different tactics – they had to get the shopkeepers on their side.

When the crowd of circus children pushed their way into MacAllan's Tailors on Princes Street, the bald, severe-looking man behind the counter stiffened on the spot. Lizzie saw his hand creeping under the counter and she clutched Malachy's arm, thinking he was going for a gun. But instead the man lifted out a knobbly stick.

'We'll no' be having any hanky-panky in my shop,' he warned them. 'If you're no' buying, then clear off.'

Lizzie licked her lips, bracing herself to ask the man if he wouldn't mind putting up a poster in his shop window. But Collette swept past her, smiling like an angel, holding the poster up. 'Would you mind putting this up, *m'sieu*? You can have some free tickets in exchange.'

The moment the man heard her charming French accent, his anger melted away. 'Free tickets, you say? And you'll be in the show?'

'But of course!'

'Well, I'm sure I could find room for a wee poster…'

'It's funny,' Lizzie whispered to Nora. 'I always think of Collette as one of us, but really she's nearly a grown-up.'

Nora nodded. 'She's eighteen. That's old enough to get married if she wants.'

As the friends strolled down Princes Street, leaving a trail of posters in windows behind them, they curtseyed or lifted their hats to the impressive-looking people who passed by them on the pavement. Lizzie hadn't known Edinburgh was a centre of fashion, but everyone she saw seemed to know how to dress. She saw smart tailcoats, silk cravats, shining toppers, and so much tweed it was like being out with a shooting party.

'All these shops are selling the same sort of cloth,' Lizzie pointed out. 'Tweeds and tartans and such.'

'Scotland's famous for wool the world over,' said Hari. 'They're proud of their fabrics here. With good reason.'

'"If it wasnae for the weavers,"' Erin sang, '"what would we do?"'

Dru paused and looked longingly into a window, where a huge selection of kilts and plaids were on display. 'I need a souvenir,' he suddenly announced. 'I am going to buy a kilt.'

Lizzie gawped at him. 'But … you've heard what they say…'

'Ah, *oui*,' said Dru. 'To wear the kilt properly, a man must wear nothing at all beneath. Let the air in, no? Very bracing.'

'Dru!' Lizzie burst out laughing as Erin and Nora flushed and giggled.

Collette just rolled her eyes. 'Always 'ee is like this,' she said, sighing. 'Trying to be the centre of attention.'

Dru shrugged. 'What's the problem? The kilt is very dashing, I think.'

'You're a high wire performer, you great twit!' Lizzie said, gasping for breath. 'What if you went up on the wire with a kilt on, and everyone saw up it?'

Malachy doubled over with laughter. 'We'd be ruined … but it might be worth it! Oh Lord, the look on people's faces!'

Just then, a noise squealed and blared into Lizzie's

ears. She jumped a foot in the air and covered her ears up. It was painful to listen to, whatever it was.

'What's that horrible racket?' she asked the others.

'It's the cry of the Loch Ness Monster!' Hari shouted above the din. 'Run for your life!'

Malachy laughed and pointed to a man on the street corner. He wore a kilt and sporran, and his red-veined cheeks bulged out like angry swellings as he blew and blew into a pipe. Under his arm was … a *thing*, and Lizzie realized that the sound was coming out of it. It seemed to be part sack, part bellows, and part plumbing.

'The Highland bagpipes,' Malachy said. 'I love 'em. The sound of the bagpipes made Scotland's enemies flee in terror before the warriors even appeared.'

'I bet it bloomin' did,' Lizzie said. 'It sounds worse than Akula the elephant when she's got a bellyache.'

Erin pointed to a crowd of people moving away up the street. 'Looks like they all agree with you.'

'Scots, running from bagpipes?' Malachy shook his head. 'Never happen. That lot are heading over to the Assembly Rooms. Must be some kind of big do on there.'

'So let's flyer 'em!' Lizzie ran to the throng of people

and began stuffing circus flyers into their hands. 'There you go, sir. Fitzy's Circus Spectacular, in Holyrood Park! Bring the kids!'

'Wee 'uns?' the baffled, bearded man said. 'I haven't got any.'

'So borrow some,' Lizzie grinned. 'Here you go, madam…'

The Penny Gaff Gang moved along the queue, passing out flyers as they went. Further down the road they passed some stern-looking people handing out flyers of their own. Lizzie took one out of curiosity. END INFANT LABOUR, it declared, along with a grisly illustration of a child being eaten alive by a machine.

'Reformists,' Malachy muttered.

Lizzie gave the man a cheerful circus flyer and a broad smile. 'Fair exchange,' she said.

Soon they reached the Assembly Rooms. Lizzie looked up at the impressive building, with its columns and porch like an ancient Greek temple and warm light shining from its tall windows. *The dear old show tent would look a bit shabby next to that*, she thought. But curiosity nudged her. Fitzy's Circus needed to pull crowds of this size. This was their competition

– what could all these people be so interested in? She approached a lady with her hands thrust into a muff the size of a baby bear.

The lady peered down at her through little half-moon glasses. 'Yes?'

'What's everyone come here to see?'

'Why, Mr Grant, of course!' The lady drew her hand out and pointed to a poster.

PUBLIC SÉANCE, the poster declared, BY MR DOUGLAS GRANT, WORLD-FAMOUS SPIRITUALIST AND MEDIUM. Lizzie stared at the picture of Grant, partly at his broad chin and vast moustache, but more at the way his feet were clearly hovering above the ground, his toes pointed downwards.

'He's flying!' Lizzie declared in amazement.

The people around her tutted, and someone muttered something about 'ruffians spoiling the vibrations'. The old lady made a face, as if she smelled something bad.

Malachy quickly pulled Lizzie away. 'They're a bit posh, this lot,' he muttered. 'Still, we ought to get inside. You could learn a lot from this Grant bloke.'

'What, like how to fly?' Lizzie said, not bothering to hide her scorn. The crowd could think what they liked.

'It's a bloomin' stage trick, that. Got to be.'

'That don't matter,' whispered Malachy. 'The money these folks are spending is real, even if his powers ain't!'

He had a point, Lizzie realized. Despite being a genuine psychic, she didn't have Grant's pulling power. Besides, how could she show people her powers were real unless she could lure them into her tent in the first place? Showmanship mattered, and this Douglas Grant obviously had cartloads of it.

'Fine. Let's get some tickets,' she said.

Nora ran up the steps past the queue to investigate, but came back shaking her head. She mouthed the words *three shillings each* to Lizzie and mimed hanging herself and sticking her tongue out.

Lizzie sighed and turned to go, but before she'd taken three steps, a soft whistle caught her attention. A handsome young man was lurking in one of the archways. He tipped his hat at her and gave a wink.

'Ticket tout,' Malachy said with a grimace.

'*Pas du tout,*' Collette said. ''Ee looks nice.'

The man beckoned them over with his finger, and without hesitating, Collette headed over to him. The others followed until they were all standing together in a side alley. The man's grin showed white teeth and made Lizzie think of foxes.

'Criminal price they're charging, eh?'

'Criminal,' Lizzie agreed.

'I'm no tout. And when I was your age, I'd have sneaked in the side entrance,' he said. 'Reckon I'm still game. How about you?'

'Lead the way,' Lizzie said, laughing.

There was nobody standing watch over the side door. The man gently turned the handle and eased the door open. Malachy moved forward, but the man stopped him. 'Ladies first, laddie.' Collette giggled as she slipped past him and into the building.

'What do we call you?' Lizzie asked.

'Call me Fergus Campbell,' he said, shaking her hand. 'You'll not have heard of me, not yet. But you will.'

As her hand touched his, a sudden image blazed across Lizzie's inner vision.

Campbell was scribbling notes by candlelight: excited, on the trail of something big. Now he was talking to a policeman, writing down more notes. And then he was proudly watching a newspaper roll off the printing press.

'You're a newspaper reporter!' Lizzie cried.

'Don't shout,' he said through his teeth, 'or they'll

be down on me like hawks. You're right, though. What was it gave me away? Inky fingers, eh?'

'Something like that,' Lizzie said, and relished his appraising look. *Let him wonder how I knew,* she thought.

With the Assembly Rooms packed to the rafters out front, it was child's play to sneak backstage and into the wings. Lizzie began to panic, certain they would be discovered, but Dru was able to shinny up a rope to an upper platform and let a rope ladder down. One by one, they clambered up into the dusty dark to a perch where they could watch the show in secrecy.

'Nobody's been up here in years!' Erin whispered.

'Ugh!' said Collette. 'Dust marks on my dress.'

'All of you, shush!' Malachy hissed.

Fergus Campbell nodded and held his notebook ready – Lizzie noticed he had suddenly become a lot more serious. Somehow, she didn't think he was here to review the show. If that was the case, he'd surely be sitting out front. No, Lizzie was sure the journalist was on the trail of a sensational story of some sort.

A tall, slender man in an evening suit walked onto the stage and strolled back and forth, straightening his cuffs and looking at his pocketwatch. 'That's him,'

Fergus whispered to her. 'Grant. The medium.'

'Two minutes to curtain, Mister Grant!' said a hoarse-voiced stagehand. The star medium gave him a vague wave of thanks, then poured a glass of water and gargled with it.

When the curtains parted, the applause began. *He ain't even done anything yet*, Lizzie thought, irritated. Grant raised his hands, modestly accepting the crowd's adoration.

'As a son of the Highlands,' he began, 'my heart leaps like a mountain stag now that I walk once more among my people.'

'He means he's glad to be home,' Hari whispered.

Grant raised a dramatic finger. A thick, velvety silence hung in the air. Nobody dared to breathe.

'They are close, my friends,' he said with a nod and a smile. 'Aye, you know of whom I speak. You need no miracles to convince you. The beloved are close ... they who the ignorant call "dead" but who we know to be simply passed over.'

Lizzie looked at the enraptured faces in the crowd – they were drinking in every word.

'Hark!' said Grant. 'Can you hear them? Do you not hear their voices, sweet as fairy bells? No? Then we must *believe*. If we become like little children in our innocence, perhaps the spirits will speak. Will you speak to us, spirits?'

The stage lights lowered to a dim glimmer, and then to near total darkness. The audience gasped – Grant's upraised hands were glowing with a faint light.

'I've heard he does this,' Fergus murmured.

Lizzie caught a whiff of something unexpected and yet familiar. The harsh, pungent smell stuck in the back of her throat. 'It's oil of phosphorus!' she said as she covered her nose and mouth. 'That's what's making the glow!'

It was cruel how smells could conjure up memories. As if it had been yesterday, Lizzie was flung back to the days when she was a little girl. Her brother, already dying from lung disease, had come staggering home every day with his clothes reeking of phosphorus.

He had worked in a match factory. Lucifer matches, they were sometimes called – and just like the Devil, they had corrupted what was good and true. The chemicals in that hellish place had destroyed his health, sending him to an early grave.

If he hadn't have worked there, though, Lizzie might be dead too – of starvation. The money her brother brought home was to feed the family, and it did, but her father stole most of it and spent it on drink. Then Lizzie's mother too had fallen ill and had slowly wasted away, coughing her last breaths into a bloody handkerchief.

'You all right, Liz?' Malachy asked. 'You look sick.'

'It's the smell,' Liz said, not wanting to say any more.

'Phosphorus oil, you reckon?' Fergus eagerly jotted down a note in his book. 'I say, look at him now. He's levitating!'

Down on the stage, Grant was indeed rising into the air. Someone in the crowd gasped out loud and fainted dead away, and a thin voice from the front row began to chant, 'Oh, we are blessed! Oh, we are blessed!' again and again, like some deranged inmate from a lunatic asylum.

'I'd heard of levitation,' Hari said softly, 'but I never expected to see it. In India, yogis practise for years and maybe lift half an inch off the ground. This is astonishing!'

Dru laughed. 'Not really. It's just another trick.'

Fergus, pencil at the ready, asked, 'How's he doing it?'

'He is standing on something … a bar, I think.'

'You're right, Dru!' Erin said. 'I can see it now too.'

Malachy said, 'It's painted black, so the audience can't see it with the lights turned down. Clever.'

The only sound up on the platform was the scratching of Fergus's pencil. 'It was my lucky day running into you lot,' he said. 'Grant's a pompous windbag. I've been looking forward to letting some of the hot air out of him.'

'Will you remember us when you are famous, Mister Campbell?' joked Collette.

Fergus glanced up at her. 'I'll remember you for the rest of my life, lass,' he said, and quickly went back to writing. Collette pretended to be embarrassed, but Lizzie could tell she was pleased.

As Grant performed trick after trick, the circus children explained to Fergus how he was doing them. Hari pointed out all the mind-reading tricks he and his uncle used, while Dru and Malachy debunked the stage magic.

Lizzie almost felt sorry for Grant. By the time Fergus Campbell had revealed his stagecraft secrets, nobody would ever trust his mediumship again. She couldn't even be sure it was right to do this to him – the audience were fools, but they believed. If they found some comfort in all this, then what was the harm in it?

'Now, my brothers and sisters, I will attempt to speak with a spirit. Someone close to one of you.' Grant slowly looked over the audience, while from somewhere an accordion played a mournful tune. Lizzie didn't like it – it sounded like funeral music.

Fergus readied his notebook. 'An actual séance? Let's see how he fakes this.'

'I would like to call for a volunteer,' said Grant. 'Is there anyone among you who wishes to speak to the dear departed?'

'Aye,' rang out a voice.

All eyes turned to look as a burly man stood up. His clothes were finely tailored and all black – the colour of mourning.

'I need to speak to my sister,' he said. 'My dead sister. On a matter of the utmost urgency.'

CHAPTER 3

'Come forward,' said Grant, smiling. 'Do not be afraid.'

The man didn't look afraid at all. He marched up the side steps in a business-like way and looked out over the crowd as if he was daring them to say something.

'Your name, sir?'

'Alexander MacDonald,' the man said.

A ripple of excitement went through the crowd. People turned to one another and whispered behind their hands. MacDonald just kept glowering, as if he'd expected this.

'Who's he?' Lizzie whispered to the young journalist.

'You've not heard of him?' Fergus said in surprise.

'He's probably the richest man in here tonight. You know what an industrialist is?'

'Someone who owns factories?'

'That's him. He owns a woollen mill – well, half of one – and he's done quite nicely out of it, thank you very much. His little niece owns the other half.' Fergus licked the tip of his pencil. 'He acts as her ward.'

'His niece,' Lizzie echoed. 'So the dead woman he wants to speak to – his sister – is her mother?'

Fergus nodded and put a finger to his lips, then pointed down to the stage.

Grant placed his hands on MacDonald's shoulders and grimaced, like a man who badly needs to go to the toilet. Lizzie nearly laughed, but managed to stop by biting the inside of her cheek.

'I sense a presence,' Grant groaned. 'Forgive me, but I must ask. How did your sister pass away?'

'She and her husband both died of cholera two years ago,' MacDonald told him. The audience murmured at that. Lizzie wondered if his matter-of-fact manner went all the way down, or if he was masking a deep grief.

'I believe you loved your sister very much,' said Grant, screwing up his face like someone crushing the last drops of juice from an orange.

MacDonald coughed. He seemed about to say something, but didn't, and Lizzie was suddenly sure that the man was more wounded inside than he wanted to say.

'I see a face!' Grant cried out. 'A face most fair and shining like an angel. But it is not the light of the sun, nor of the moon that lights her perfect face. It is the light of love that shines from her. Your sister is here, sir. She is beside you even as I speak.'

The audience applauded. Lizzie sat stock-still, feeling sick. Why were they clapping him? Couldn't they tell he was just making up the sort of drivel they wanted to hear?

'You can see her?' MacDonald asked. Lizzie saw he was clenching his fists, so as not to cry in front of everyone.

'Clear as day,' Grant said with a soft smile. 'I see her flowing hair, and her perfect white skin, and the smile she is giving her dear brother, Alexander. My good man, if only you could see what I am seeing now.'

'Well, that's convincing,' Nora said sarcastically. '"Your sister had hair and skin!"'

Fergus chuckled.

'I bet her name began with a letter of the alphabet too,' said Erin.

'She whispers her name,' Grant said. 'A beautiful name, like the summer flowers. Fiona … no, Flora! Was your sister's name Flora?'

'Aye, it was.'

There were gasps from the audience.

Fergus raised a questioning eyebrow. 'What do we make of that?'

'He probably knew already,' Malachy said. 'This bloke MacDonald is famous, ain't he?'

Grant's voice drew you in. It was soothing and encouraging, and it was easy to believe him. Just for a moment, Lizzie wondered if he really did have powers like hers, even if he wrapped it all up in a lot of stagecraft.

Then, without warning, her own powers surged to life. In her mind's eye, she saw Alexander MacDonald's sister. She was running away from him, down the side of Arthur's Seat, laughing…

'Wait, Flora!' MacDonald shouted, already out of breath, but Flora wasn't waiting. 'Catch me if you can, Pickles!' she called.

As soon as she saw Flora's face, Lizzie knew Grant

was nothing but a faker. Perfect white skin, eh? Flora's face was covered with freckles – so many that it looked like an artist had applied each one with a little brush. In the vision, Flora was so alive and full of fun that it hurt Lizzie's heart to think of her being dead and buried.

'Don't worry, Flora,' Lizzie muttered under her breath. 'I won't let him get away with conning your brother.'

Grant kept on gushing about Flora's love and how she was watching over her brother like an angel, while MacDonald answered his questions. Yes, there was a special place where they used to go together. Yes, there was a little child she had left behind – well, everyone knew that, it seemed. Just because Grant had recently returned from America didn't mean he couldn't pick up a newspaper.

'Look at how he's holding MacDonald's hands,' Hari pointed out. 'It's so he can feel every tiny movement MacDonald makes. That's called cold reading. You make guesses, and if the person flinches away, you know you're on the wrong track.'

'More trickery,' Fergus said, jotting that down.

'It's ruddy disgusting,' Lizzie said. 'That man's in

mourning. He's desperate. He wants to believe his sister's in a better place, but Grant's just feeding him a pack of lies! And it's all for money, and to show off!'

'Hear, hear,' said Fergus.

'He's nothing but a fraud,' Lizzie seethed.

Fergus frowned. 'Of course he's a fraud. Didn't you know? There's no such thing as a psychic – they're *all* scammers and con men.'

'You want to take that back, mate,' Malachy said, shoving a circus flyer at Fergus. 'We've got a real psychic at Fitzy's.'

'*The Magnificent Lizzie Brown*,' Fergus read. 'Who came up with that? She sounds like a cleaning woman.'

'It's her real name,' Malachy said. 'Everything about her is real.'

'So who is she?'

The Penny Gaff Gang all silently pointed to Lizzie.

Fergus swallowed. 'You? *You're* the "magnificent" Lizzie Brown?' He glanced at the flyer. 'Genuine clairvoyant, dozens of testimonials?'

'That's right.'

'You'll forgive me if I'm sceptical, I hope.'

Lizzie glared right back at Fergus, who was looking at her with a suspicious frown.

'You can put me to the test any time you like, mate,' she said. If Fergus thought he had another Grant on his hands, she'd happily show him just how wrong he was.

Grant talked a lot about very little. MacDonald returned to the audience, looking 'like a man who'd lost a shilling and found sixpence' as Nora put it; not unhappy, but not exactly content, either.

After that, there came a 'lecture', which turned out to be an hour of twaddle about the spirit world. Grant very seriously spoke of 'higher vibrations' and 'celestial layers' until Lizzie's head spun.

He's making it all sound so complicated, she thought. *That must be part of the scam. Baffle 'em until they don't know whether they're coming or going.*

'It's so much easier the way I do it,' she whispered to Malachy. 'I see a spirit, and I talk to 'em. That's that. Plain as potatoes.'

Grant finally left, to a standing ovation. A tiny, wizened old man took the stage at the end of the show. 'He looks like a gnome,' Erin said happily.

'I'd like to thank Mr Grant, and to remind members

of the Spiritualist Society…' he wheezed.

'Speak up!' someone shouted.

'…that there will be a fairy hunt and picnic on Sunday.'

Lizzie shook her head. 'This place is full of loonies,' she muttered. 'How can some grown-ups actually believe that fairies exist? Fairy hunt indeed.'

Dru looked down the rope ladder. 'We'd better get out of here, *mes amis*, before the stagehands find us.'

Like a gang of robbers, they clambered down and hurried through the building one by one, glancing over their shoulders and peering around corners. Lizzie was worried the side door would be locked, but it opened on the first try.

'Phew,' Malachy said, once they were all out. 'Back to the circus?'

Lizzie shook her head. 'I have to talk to Alexander MacDonald.' Without waiting to see if the others would follow, she ran round to the front of the theatre, where the excited crowds were leaving.

There was MacDonald, straightening his tie amid a throng of posh-looking people. 'What a privilege, to join Mr Grant himself on stage!' cooed the elderly woman Lizzie had spoken to before. MacDonald gave her a curt nod, but looked impatient to be away.

Lizzie dived into the crowd, pushing and elbowing her way through. 'I say!' gasped a man with a monocle as Lizzie trod on his foot. *Never mind them*, she thought. She had a mission.

'Mister MacDonald!' she shouted, jumping up and waving over the crowd's heads. He didn't see her. She cursed and fought her way through. A wealthy man's fat belly squashed up against her like a sweaty pillow.

MacDonald was leaving. She lunged for his arm and grabbed his sleeve. 'Sir?'

'Let go!'

'I need to speak to you.'

'I don't give hand-outs, girl. And I'm a very busy man.' He tugged himself out of her grip.

'Grant is a fraud!' she yelled. 'He didn't see nothin'. He couldn't tell you nothin'. He *lied*. And you know it!'

Gasps, shouts, cries of alarm from all around her. Lizzie didn't care. She stood her ground until MacDonald turned around to look at her curiously.

'What is the meaning of this?' he said.

'I'm a psychic,' she said quickly, while she had his attention. 'A real one. Come to Fitzy's circus and I'll give you a proper reading.' She pressed a flyer into his hand and closed his fingers around it.

MacDonald gave a short, sharp laugh. 'A rival psychic, eh? Why on earth should I consult you?'

The crowd had backed away from Lizzie now. They whispered to each other as if she was dangerous, and one of them hissed at her, like a child booing a pantomime villain. She spun round and gave them a look of total contempt, as if they were something she'd wipe off her shoe, then turned back to MacDonald.

'Why should you consult me? Because I know what it's like to lose someone you love,' she said savagely. 'My mum died, and my brother. I'd never use someone else's grief to make money like that Grant does – it ain't right!'

MacDonald pondered that. He glanced at the flyer she'd given him. 'Fitzy's Circus?'

'Come see me there. No charge. And bring something that belonged to your sister.'

MacDonald sighed and shook his head. He closed his fist on the flyer, crumpling it. 'I see no reason to believe you.'

Lizzie took a breath. 'Flora would want you to … *Pickles*.'

His face froze in total shock. 'How … how did

you know my sister called me *Pickles*? I never told anybody that.'

'I told you,' she said. 'I'm not a fraud. I'm for real.'

'And who, may I enquire, are you calling a fraud?' It was Grant, marching angrily through the crowd that parted for him like the Red Sea. 'I'd check your pockets, sir. Make sure she hasn't picked them.'

'I ain't no thief,' Lizzie growled. 'Not like some people.'

Grant glared down at her, bristling. 'Ushers!' he bellowed. 'Someone call the ushers!'

Two large, uniformed men came running up. 'Mister Grant?'

'Take this scruffy little urchin and escort her from the premises. Good and far. Toss her in the River Leith if you have to.' Grant pressed a coin into an usher's hand, and Lizzie saw it gleamed gold. 'No need to be gentle.'

'Right you are, Mister Grant.' Together, the ushers stepped forward, reaching for Lizzie. They grabbed her, one holding onto each arm, and hoisted her kicking and screaming off the ground.

'Oh, look,' said the man with the monocle. 'The urchin's levitating.'

Grant guffawed at that and slapped him heartily on the back.

Lizzie struggled and tried to kick the ushers. 'Let me go! Put me down!' But it was no good. They manhandled her down the steps, banging her knee agonizingly on a marble bollard. Lizzie saw Dru and the others running up towards her.

Dru rolled a sleeve up, showing a muscular forearm. 'Get your hands off her, *crétin*,' he said.

'Or you'll do what?' the usher sneered.

'You're a pair of filthy cowards!' shrieked Collette. 'How dare you treat a young girl that way?'

The other usher whistled at her. 'French girls. Ain't they pretty when they're angry?'

Both the ushers forced their way through the Penny Gaff Gang, sneering and spitting insults. Then they stopped dead. Fergus the reporter had stepped into their path.

'If I were you I'd step aside, *sir*,' the usher said.

'Fergus Campbell, *Edinburgh Gazette*.' Fergus took out his notepad and tapped the pencil against his nose thoughtfully. 'What headline do you think works best? "Uniformed ogres given the sack", or "Usher brutes drummed out of a job"?'

'What's he saying?' demanded the other.

'I'll make it plain as a pikestaff, my laddie-bucks,' said Fergus. 'Let the wee girl go, or so help me God I'll have you up before the Bench on a charge of wanton and unnecessary force. And believe me, you'll be guilty in the eyes of the public before you even go to trial. I'll see to it.'

The ushers dumped Lizzie on the pavement and ran back inside without a backward glance. Fergus offered her his hand to help her up.

'Ta,' she said. 'I owe you one, mate.'

'Ach, some people turn into right little Caesars the moment they put on a uniform. They just need putting back in their place.'

Collette curtseyed. 'They say French gentlemen are the most *galant*, but now I see that Scottish gentlemen can be knights in shining armour too.'

Fergus blustered. 'Steady on. No need to go that far.' But Lizzie saw that he was blushing.

'Come on,' she said, and dusted herself down. 'Back to the circus. We've got some thinking to do.'

'And I've an article to write.' Fergus waved from the street corner. 'Cheerio for now. Something tells me we'll see each another again…'

CHAPTER 4

On Grand Opening Day, Ma Sullivan's tea tent always served a special breakfast to 'set the performers up'. The usual gallons of tea and bowlfuls of porridge were joined by plates heaped with crackly bacon, slice upon slice of golden-brown toast, eggs, fruit and whatever local dishes Ma Sullivan had found.

This morning, Lizzie was amazed to find steaming peppery meat puddings among the fare on offer. 'That's haggis,' Mario the strong man explained. His curly moustache twitched up in a big smile as he helped himself to four of them.

'What's in it?'

'Sheep's lungs, minced up. Tastes a lot better than it sounds, trust me.'

Lizzie tasted it. He was right – the stuff had a strong, hearty flavour that somehow left you wanting more.

Malachy and Hari shuffled over to make room at their table. 'Morning, Liz!' Malachy poured her some tea. 'We were just talking about you.'

'What did you think of Grant's act?' Hari asked.

Lizzie shrugged. 'Not much. He was a fraud.'

'Yes,' said Malachy, 'but didn't he sell it well? If you'd put any other bloke up there, talking the claptrap he was coming out with, he'd have been laughed off the stage! Total confidence, that's how he does it.'

'So we were thinking,' said Hari. 'If a little stage magic works so well for a fake medium, then what might it do for a real one?'

Lizzie slurped her tea. 'Oh, here we go. You two have been plottin' again, ain't you?'

'Just think about it, Liz!' Malachy pleaded. 'What's the harm in a bit of flash and dazzle? You're still giving a real reading at the end of it.'

'It might even help the customers relax, and put their trust in you,' added Hari.

'You two should do a double act, if you know

so much about it,' Lizzie said with a scowl.

Malachy held up a finger. 'Hear me out. What if … just for the sake of argument … you did a levitation act in the show tent, to open the performance?'

'We could use wires!' Hari said as Lizzie looked at him in horror. 'Like when fairies need to fly in a stage show.'

'You'd be perfectly safe.'

'Beat Grant at his own game!' Malachy's eyes were bright.

'Not a chance,' Lizzie said. 'For one, I ain't a performer. I tried that once, when I had to step in for Erin after she hurt her arm, remember?'

'You did all right,' Hari said.

'I ain't doing that again,' Lizzie said, shaking her head. 'And for two, I ain't a fraud. I don't need no tricks!'

'So you'll consider it, then?' Malachy said.

Before Lizzie could yell at him, Nora burst into the tea tent and made straight for the table where one of her older brothers, Sean, was sitting. 'Are you ever going to grow up, Sean Sullivan?' she shouted.

Sean shot up out of his seat like a jack-in-the-box. 'What's rattled your cage, Nora?'

His sister brandished her riding costume and showed him where the buttons used to be. 'Pullin' my buttons off, on opening day and all? You're a disgrace.'

Sean flung up his hands. 'It wasn't me!'

'"It wasn't me!"' Nora mocked. 'Six years old if he's a day. Why'd you *do* these things?'

Ma Sullivan laid a heavy hand on Nora's shoulder. 'Sit down, the both of you. Nora, let your brother alone.'

'But, Ma!'

'Hush. This is my fault, and I'll make it right.'

'Your fault?' Sean echoed.

'That milk I left out for the fairies was on the turn,' Ma Sullivan sighed. 'They must have taken offence and plucked your buttons off.'

'Oh no!' wailed Nora.

Ma Sullivan took the costume and pondered. 'There's time enough to mend it. Tonight I'll lay out fresh milk, and bake a new loaf just for the fairies. That should make amends.'

Lizzie couldn't believe it. A grown-up, talking about fairies in such a serious way? She couldn't help it – she laughed out loud, and some of her tea went down the wrong way, leaving her coughing helplessly while Ma

Sullivan gave her a long, knowing look. It seemed to say *I told you so*.

The grand performances were what the posters advertised, but the time before and between shows was Lizzie's time to shine. The sideshows and penny gaffs needed to keep people entertained while they waited for the main show to start. A circus this size, Fitzy always said, had to have something happening all the time. 'Keep the heart beating and the cash trickling in,' he would say.

Lizzie's fortune-telling tent was waiting for her, striped purple and black, with a lovely hand-painted signboard outside covered in swirly golden writing. She dressed in her mystic robes, lit some incense, then laid out her crystal ball and tarot cards. Of course, she didn't need any of these things to have visions – but customers expected a fortune-teller's tent to look a certain way. Once everything was ready, Lizzie sat down to wait for her first customer. This part was always a quiet thrill, as you never knew who you were going to get.

She jumped in surprise as the tent flap was flung

back. A tall, haggard man in a frock coat stood there with staring eyes and bared teeth. 'You're the fortune-teller, aye?'

'I am,' she said, doing her best to sound calm and wise after the shock.

'Right. Ticketty-flaming-boo. Let's part the mystic veil and see what the future holds, eh?' He gave her a ghoulish grin and stuck his hand out. 'Go on, girl. I don't bite.'

Lizzie wasn't sure whether to believe him but she took his hand anyway. After the reading was over, he left her a generous tip.

She hoped that her next customer would be a bit less eccentric, but Edinburgh seemed to be full of bizarre characters. She read the palms of a pointy-nosed schoolmistress, a baffled man in a kilt who claimed to be an inventor, a stocky bearded fellow who was convinced Lizzie could tell him where to find some buried treasure, and a ginger-haired tomboy who was going to run away to sea instead of getting married.

'Phew,' she said. 'I'm worn out after that lot.' She stepped out of her tent, thinking she'd reach the show tent just in time for the main performance to start.

To her surprise Alexander MacDonald, the man

from the public séance, was waiting outside. He had an uncertain look on his face.

'You said to come,' he explained.

Lizzie glanced at the show tent, then held her own tent open for him. 'Come in.'

MacDonald sat, and unwrapped a black fan with great care. 'This belonged to Flora,' he said. 'Nobody else has touched it since she died. Not even me.'

'I'll have to, I'm afraid. That's how it works.'

He nodded. 'I asked you a question, but you never answered. How did you know she called me Pickles?'

'I saw you together,' Lizzie said.

'How?'

'I don't know how I see things. I just do. The visions … it's like they're given to me.'

'Douglas Grant says the same thing,' Macdonald said. 'You claim you're not a fraud. Very well. Prove it.'

Lizzie's heart beat hard. She touched the fan, feeling its lacquered wood, stroking its soft feathers. Every single time she did this, she felt a moment of panic. *What if nothing happens?*

But something did happen. In the darkness behind her closed eyes, Flora appeared.

Her long hair floated around her, as if she was

underwater. An uncanny light shone from her eyes, but Lizzie felt no fear.

'Hello, ma'am,' Lizzie said.

'Can you see her?' Macdonald said urgently. 'Is she well?'

Flora laughed. *'Same old Pickles. Always fretting! Bless his heart.'*

Lizzie repeated everything Flora said. MacDonald's face crumpled and he sagged in his chair, as he let go of a weight he'd carried for years and years. 'That's her,' he whispered.

'Tell Alexander I love him very much,' Flora went on, *'and I am so proud of him. I watch over him and my little Amelia every day. He is the kindest, most generous uncle she could ever wish for, even if he does have knobbly knees.'*

At that, MacDonald made a noise that was half-laugh and half-sob.

'Our father would be proud of him too, I know. He has made our family business grow stronger than ever.'

Suddenly Flora's face grew serious and a sinister feeling washed over Lizzie. *'But heed to my words, and be sure to pass them on: Beware the fairy!'*

Lizzie opened her mouth to speak, but before any sound could come out, the tent door was flung open and the bright light of day flooded in.

Instantly the connection was broken. Flora's image vanished like a reflection in a pool when a rock is thrown in it and MacDonald sat up with a start, his eyes wet.

Lizzie began to yell, 'I'm in the middle of a reading—'

Then she stopped herself mid-sentence. Standing in the doorway was a little girl, probably no more than five years old, with honey-coloured hair that fell down past her shoulders in thick curls. Her face had a mischievous smile that Lizzie found familiar, just as she recognized the dusting of freckles across the girl's nose.

'Amelia!' MacDonald exclaimed. 'Your uncle Ally's very busy in here – I'm sorry, Miss Brown, she's always getting in and out of places – *oof*!'

Amelia had grabbed MacDonald's sleeve and now she tugged him hard, like a disobedient puppy. 'You *have* to come, Uncle Ally, because it is *very* important.' With a glance at Lizzie, she told her uncle in a loud whisper, 'It is a special thing! The specialest thing ever!'

She takes after her mother, Lizzie thought. 'What have you seen, Miss Amelia?'

Ignoring her, Amelia bounced up and down on the spot, flapping her arms as if she was about to explode.

'What is it, darling?' said MacDonald.

'I saw a *fairy*. A real live one. She can fly in the air! A fairy, Uncle! Come and see!'

Flora's warning surged back into Lizzie's mind. 'Mister MacDonald, I need to tell you—'

'Oh, she's no' in here, is she?' came a voice from outside. A sturdy, red-haired young woman in dark clothes entered the tent. She rolled her eyes when she saw Amelia. 'I'm so sorry to interrupt, sir. I took my eyes off her for one second and off she'd gone.'

Amelia burst into giggles and dived underneath the table, peeping out from behind the velvet drape like a little caged animal. 'You can't find me, Maisie.'

'Come on out now,' Amelia's nursemaid said with gentle sternness. 'We can play hide and seek back at the house. But we don't play it at the circus! What if you'd run off and hidden in the lion's cage, eh?'

'Leo would have gobbled you all up!' Lizzie said, making her fingers into claws. Amelia squealed and gave Lizzie a huge smile.

'Out,' Maisie repeated. She held out her hand.

Amelia heaved a dramatic sigh and came out from under the table.

'That's better. Now come along. You don't want to

miss the rest of the show, do you?'

'Come and see my fairy, Uncle Ally!' yelled the girl. Macdonald hurried after her, and all three of them left Lizzie's tent. She glanced at where he'd been sitting, and then had to look again. A gold sovereign lay on the velvet tablecloth – it hadn't been there before.

Lizzie picked it up, marvelling at its weight. Nobody had ever paid so much for a reading before. 'And they say the Scots are tight-fisted,' she murmured as she pocketed it. 'I reckon I win this one, Mister Douglas Grant!'

But … she still hadn't passed on Flora's warning, she realized. And Amelia was dragging her uncle and nursemaid off to see a fairy. Or something she *thought* was a fairy.

Fairies weren't real, though. So how could she pass on such a stupid warning? MacDonald might laugh in her face.

No, Lizzie knew she needed to tell them, silly as it sounded. There might still be time to reach them. She ran for the show tent.

* * *

Amelia was safe. Lizzie saw her sitting in the front row, with Maisie on one side and her uncle on the other. There was no way to get closer – the seats were all packed – but Lizzie could at least crouch down uncomfortably and watch from the aisle.

The lights were turned down low, and a breathless hush hung over the circus. They were between acts. The audience was waiting for someone to appear.

Next moment, Amelia's voice rang out:

'There's my fairy!' Amelia yelled. 'Bootiful fairy lady. Hello!'

The audience around her laughed. Cymbals clashed. It was Collette, swinging high above their heads on the trapeze, caught in a beam of light from the whale-oil lanterns. She waved to Amelia and gave her a dazzling smile.

Lizzie felt sweet relief. So *that* was the fairy. Collette did look like she was flying, and her dress streamed with white taffeta that looked a bit like wings. If you were only five years old, your imagination filled in a lot of details.

Lizzie crept to the back of the stalls and settled down to watch the show. Now she knew Amelia was in no immediate danger, passing on Flora's message didn't seem so urgent. Like his little niece, Alexander MacDonald was watching the trapeze act, utterly entranced. Lizzie suddenly realized what the warning might mean: Flora was warning her brother not to fall in love with Collette, the 'fairy'. He wouldn't have been the first man to fall under the beautiful trapeze artist's spell, Lizzie knew.

'Thank you one and all, and goodnight!' Fitzy said, sweeping his arm around in a deep bow. 'Do come again, and remember to tell your friends!'

Lizzie clapped along with everyone else. It had been a superb first show, one of the best she could remember ... even if the audience here were a bit keen on shouting advice at the performers – she hadn't expected the bellow of 'GET STUCK INTAE HIM!' during the clown fight!

She ran down to join Amelia and her family before they could leave. 'Would you like to meet your fairy?' she asked her.

'Can I, Uncle Ally?' Amelia begged. 'Please?'

MacDonald checked his watch. 'Very well. Just for

a wee while, mind.'

While the audience emptied out of the show tent, the performers came back in, laughing and congratulating one another. Collette gasped to see little Amelia sprinting up to her. 'Hello, *ma petite*! Did you wave to me?'

'I did. I saw you up in the air. You are very pretty.'

'Why, thank you! I think you are pretty too.'

'Teach me how to fly,' Amelia demanded.

'*Helas*, I cannot, for that is a fairy secret.' Collette winked to Lizzie. 'But if you wish, you may have a bounce … ?'

Collette lifted the delighted girl up to the safety net. As she set her on the net, Lizzie noticed the performer wincing slightly.

'Bouncing!' Amelia shouted, and the great net twanged and shook under her, flinging her up again and again under the circus lights.

Collette laughed and clapped, then clutched her back. Lizzie was by her side in an instant. 'What's the matter with your back?'

'Ah, it is not much. Just years of performing.' Collette smiled, and though there was pain in her face, there was no regret.

'But you're only eighteen.'

'*Oui*. We start early in our family. I had a fall when I was fifteen, and my back has never been quite right since then.'

'Bouncing!' yelled Amelia as she shot up over their heads, then fell back down again.

Maisie reached up to her. 'Right, my wee fairy child, that's quite enough bouncing for one night. It's past your bedtime.'

As the nursemaid lifted Amelia down, Lizzie saw the middle finger on Maisie's left hand was missing. Only a little stub of knuckle remained. She turned away, refusing to stare – Fitzy's Circus was full of unusual-looking people, and Lizzie had long ago trained herself out of the impolite habit of staring.

Amelia tugged Colette's dress. 'I will come and fly with you in my dreams,' she said, grinning.

'I would like that very much.'

Amelia waved goodbye, Maisie nodded politely and MacDonald lifted his hat. The next moment, all three of them were gone.

Lizzie stood and fingered the gold sovereign in her pocket. Flora's words kept coming back to her. *Beware the fairy.* She had the nagging feeling she should have passed the warning on, after all.

'But there's no such thing as fairies!' she said to herself.

Even coming from a spirit, it couldn't be a *real* warning ... could it?

CHAPTER 5

Lizzie was barely out of bed the next morning before Malachy called round to her caravan. 'I've had some ideas,' he said from outside while she dressed. 'Levitation is old hat. They'll all be doing it soon. But I reckon I can cook up some stuff that'll look like glowing ectoplasm!'

Lizzie had heard of ectoplasm – a sort of goo that ghosts used to take on a physical form. Her caravan door was in two halves, and she opened the top half now, like a window. 'I already said no. I ain't a fraud.'

'All right,' said Malachy, undeterred. 'What about shadow puppets? We could have you surrounded by dancing devils, skeletons, all sorts…'

'What part of *no* ain't you understanding?'

Someone coughed. They both turned to look. It was Fergus the journalist, standing back with an amused look on his face. 'Hope I'm not interrupting.'

'Interrupting?' Malachy said. 'If we didn't know who you were, we'd have you for trespassing! This part of the camp's for circus people only.'

Fergus laughed. 'Since when did I ever use the main entrance?'

'Don't mind Mally,' Lizzie said, coming out of the carvan, now dressed in her mystic robes for the day's work. 'He's looking out for us. Just like his father.'

'I was hoping to speak to your father, as it happens,' said Fergus. Out came the notebook and the pen. 'What with Fitzy's Circus being such a success, I thought I might do a wee piece on you. Behind the scenes at the great attraction, that sort of thing.'

Lizzie and Malachy looked at one another. 'I suppose we could show him around,' Malachy said.

'It could be good publicity,' agreed Lizzie. 'Besides, we do owe him one after last night.'

'So, where do you want to start?'

'Have you got any lions?' said Fergus. 'I've always wanted to meet a lion.'

'No touching,' Hari warned. 'He'll have your arm off.'

Leo was asleep in his cage, his great golden-furred chest rising and falling. Fergus jotted down notes. 'He's dangerous, then?'

'Deadly.'

Lizzie knew Leo was old and toothless and about as dangerous as a kitten, but she kept quiet. One of Leo's paws was dangling out of the cage bars and Hari showed Fergus how the huge sabre-like claws came out when the paw was squeezed. Fergus whistled softly.

Then the journalist shrieked. Something was scrabbling up his leg, something with a dark furry body and spindly clutching arms. He staggered back while the creature climbed him like a tree. It swung from his forearm, jumped and landed on his shoulder. 'Get it off me!' he yelled. 'Get it off!'

Leo, woken by the noise, blinked his amber eyes and stirred.

'It's only a monkey,' laughed Hari. 'Just keep still. He won't hurt you.'

Embarrassed by his outburst, Fergus did as Hari told him and Hanu peered into his eyes, sizing him up. 'Hello there,' the reporter said, a little nervous still. He tucked his pen into his pocket and patted the monkey on the head.

Hanu promptly whipped the expensive pen back out, jumped down to the ground, and ran off with it.

'Hey!' Fergus yelled, but it did no good. The monkey climbed up the bars of the lion's cage and perched up there, turning his prize over in his little hands. He chittered at Fergus. Lizzie could have sworn he was laughing.

'Sorry about that,' Hari laughed. 'He's named after a god, but he's a bit of a demon.'

Fergus shrugged and took another pen from inside his coat. 'He's not the first pickpocket I've had to deal with. But he's definitely the smallest.'

Once Hari had introduced all the animals and Fergus had made notes and sketches, the four of them moved on to the show tent. Fitzy was watching the rehearsals with his back to them.

'Come on in, Mister Campbell,' he said without turning around. 'Take a seat and make yourself at home. Just don't get in the way.'

Fergus sat in the front row, only inches from where the clowns were rehearsing a slapstick routine, and took off his hat. 'You were expecting me then, sir?'

A note of frost crept into Fitzy's voice. 'We saw you coming, if that's what you mean. Nothing happens in this circus without me hearing about it. Especially not a visit from a journalist. I was going to have you thrown out, but I was persuaded otherwise.' Fitzy pointed with his golden baton to where Collette was sitting nearby. She gave Fergus a shy wave and a little smile.

Fergus stood up abruptly. 'If I'm not welcome…'

Fitzy turned to face him, his hands behind his back. 'My people are loyal, Mister Campbell. The newspapers haven't always been our friends.'

'I assure you, I'm not here looking for scandal.'

Fitzy nodded, apparently satisfied. 'I hope you're a man of your word. But just in case … Collette? Kindly keep an eye on this man for me.'

'*Oui*, Fitzy.' Collette came over and sat next to Fergus, her legs crossed demurely. Fergus coughed and kept his eyes fixed on the clowns.

As Fitzy turned back, Lizzie saw a wicked, familiar twinkle in his eye. As always, the ringmaster knew *exactly* what he was doing.

For the next hour, they watched the acts rehearse. Once the clowns were done, Fitzy himself put Leo the lion through his paces in the lion-taming act. Next, the Sullivan boys rode their ponies wildly around the ring, firing revolvers or hurling tomahawks at targets with pinpoint accuracy. After them, the acrobats took the stage, clambering up one another's bodies to stand in gravity-defying formations.

'What do you think, *Monsieur* Reporter?' Collette teased.

'Call me Fergus, please,' he said. He looked hot and bothered, but not in any hurry to leave.

Collette put her hand to her mouth. 'Perhaps when we are better acquainted.'

'*Mademoiselle,*' said Fergus, 'I should like nothing better. An interview, perhaps. Would you mind?'

Pierre Boisset, Collette's father, chose that moment to come striding over. 'Collette! Are you going to make with the chit-chat all day?'

'But Papa, Fitzy said I was to chaperone the reporter—'

'It is time to rehearse.' Pierre glowered at Fergus. 'The reporter will just have to fend for himself.'

Collette skipped off. '*Helas*, the interview will have to wait,' she called over her shoulder. 'Perhaps another day.'

'Tomorrow?' Fergus suggested, with a boldness that made Collette blush. Pierre stiffened, but said nothing.

'This is better than being at the theatre,' Lizzie whispered to Malachy. 'I'm on the edge of me seat!'

Moments later, Fergus was watching the Astonishing Boissets perform. Despite the safety net, he looked worried for Collette's safety and spent more time chewing his knuckle nervously than writing in his notebook. Lizzie thought it was sweet. Then, with a start, she thought: *Is that what I look like, watching Dru? No wonder people tease me about liking him, if it's that obvious.*

After the Boissets, it was Nora and Erin's turn to practise. 'Since you're here,' Nora told Fergus, 'we're going to give you an exclusive!'

'Our latest trick, never before seen,' Erin added, with a proud toss of the head. 'We're calling it the "Highland Fling".'

'Ready when you are!' Dru called, dangling upside-down from a trapeze by his knees. Lizzie stared open-mouthed. For variety, acts sometimes crossed over with one another – a clown blundering through the acrobats or an elephant invading the clowns – but she'd never seen Dru take part in the

Sullivan Twins' equestrian routine before.

The first part of the stunt began. Erin and Nora cantered around the ring while Dru swung back and forth, building up momentum. Slowly both twins rose to a standing position, arms outstretched, smiling and waving.

'I wonder why they call it the Highland Fling?' Fergus wondered aloud.

Next second, they found out. As Dru swung past over Erin's head, she leaped up into the air and he caught her by the arms. He swung with her back and forth overhead while Nora continued to ride around the ring.

'Oh my gawd!' Lizzie cried. 'He's not going to—'

Dru flung Erin through the air.

Lizzie could hardly bear to watch. She imagined Erin landing on the ground and horse's hooves trampling her broken body, blood pouring out onto the sawdust.

But Nora rode into position, caught her sister around the waist and set her down gently in front of her, smiling all the while. As they galloped around the ring, the band blew a fanfare and Lizzie, Malachy and Fergus all leaped to their feet and clapped until their hands hurt. The Sullivan Twins reined their horse to a gentle stop, while Hari took care of Erin's now riderless horse.

'What did you think?' Nora called, breathless and laughing.

'I think you should perform for the Queen,' Fergus said, 'because that was incredible.'

Ma Sullivan came in with a working lunch for everyone: cheese, oat cakes and tea. The circus crew sat in the stalls, munching and chatting. The Penny Gaff Gang sat in a circle around Fergus, eager to answer his questions.

Lizzie could tell something was troubling him, though. 'Go on, spit it out,' she eventually said.

'I have to ask,' Fergus said. 'Aren't you all a bit young to be working?'

'What do you mean?' Malachy snapped.

'No offence, but—'

'But nothing,' Malachy snarled. 'We're all over ten years old.'

'You ought to be worrying about kids going up

chimneys and down mine shafts, mate,' warned Erin. 'Not us.'

Lizzie nodded. She remembered how exhausted her brother had been when he would come home from the matchstick factory. He'd told her about little children as young as five years old working ten hours a day there, in dangerous conditions.

'My dad looks after everyone who works here!' Malachy was really angry now, Lizzie saw with alarm. She tried to make him sit back down, but he wouldn't. He shook off her hand.

Fergus said in smooth tones, 'I'm not calling you a liar, young man. But some of you do very dangerous stunts. And a travelling circus complying with employment law? It's hard to believe.'

'Complying with *all* the laws,' Malachy said. 'I know what you're suggesting, mister. It's in all the papers, ain't it? The Labour Reform Movement—'

'They're good people,' Lizzie interrupted. 'The reformists are against little kids having to work in factories – that sort of thing.' The flyer she'd been given outside the Assembly Rooms had explained that the reformists were trying to make new laws to stop children under the age of ten from working in factories.

Fergus gave Lizzie a grateful nod. 'Aye, I'm a reformist. Proud to be. If you'd seen the conditions some of these industrialists force children to work in, you would be too.'

'I *have* seen them,' Lizzie said. 'My brother died from working in a matchstick factory.'

Malachy sat back down. 'Sorry, Lizzie,' he mumbled. 'But this reporter don't have no right to doubt my dad.'

As if on cue, Fitzy strode back into the show tent. His face was red with anger, and Lizzie thought he might be about to punch Fergus in the face, but the anger wasn't meant for him.

'Joey? Bungo? Front and centre – NOW!'

The two roustabouts he'd called came tramping up in front of him, one whiskery, the other hairless. 'Yes, boss?'

'How many exits does this tent have?'

The whole tent fell silent. Mouthfuls of food went unchewed. All eyes were on Fitzy and the two men standing motionless in front of him.

'Well, um, there's the main entrance.' Bungo rubbed his moustache. 'And the performers' entrance, and the side exit, for emergencies.'

'Point to the side exit,' said Fitzy.

Bungo pointed and Lizzie instantly saw what Fitzy was angry about, and a cold thud of fear hit her in the chest. A stack of pasteboard scenery, painted to look like mountains, had been dumped in front of the exit, blocking it completely. It was from the elephants' performance, in which one of the clowns played Hannibal crossing the Alps.

Fitzy narrowed his eyes. 'Are you sure that's the side exit? Only from where I'm standing, *it looks like a pile of scenery!*'

'It was only going to be there a minute, Fitzy,' Joey protested.

That was a mistake; Lizzie saw it immediately.

'Only a minute,' Fitzy repeated in a small, slow voice.

Lizzie gulped. Fitzy was like a kettle, Ma Sullivan often said. He made a lot of noise as he got hotter, but you knew he was really boiling when he went suddenly quiet. And right now he was so quiet nobody dared to breathe.

'All of you, listen,' he said. 'Ever heard of Philip Astley's amphitheatre? First circus ever created, back in 1777. First one to burn down too. He opened the Royal Amphitheatre after that. That burned down an'all.' Fitzy strode back and forth. 'And let's not forget Her Majesty's Theatre, burned to a cinder only a few years ago. You see, fire spreads very quickly, and a whole circus can go up in next to no time. It only takes a minute.' He glared at Joey. '*Only a minute.* Are you with me?'

Joey, too shamefaced to speak, stared at his feet.

'MOVE!' Fitzy bellowed.

Bungo, Joey and several other members of the crew quickly ran to remove the scenery from the exit. Lizzie watched Fergus nod in approval, write something in his notebook and underline it twice.

The last stage of the tour saw Fergus alone with Lizzie in the fortune-telling tent.

'Poor old Douglas Grant didn't convince me,' Fergus said, offering his palm, 'so let's see how you do.'

Lizzie found his life line. In most people it was a simple crease across the palm, but Fergus's zigzagged like a lightning bolt. *Bad beginnings leading to a bright future*, she thought.

As she traced her finger down his palm, images

danced before her eyes. Lizzie described what she was seeing as pictures floated by in soap-bubbles. They were cloudy, which meant they represented the distant past.

There was Fergus as a cheeky young boy, visiting the printing press with his father. There he was again as a young adult, with a red-faced editor slamming his story down onto a spike. Young Fergus winced as his editor snarled, 'You won't earn a penny from scribbling trash like this.'

The Fergus in front of her turned pale. 'How'd you do that?' he said. 'Must have been a lucky guess.'

Lizzie concentrated. A new, crystal-clear image appeared before her. She was seeing the future now. An older Fergus with ginger mutton-chop whiskers was accepting an award shaped like a golden shield. Images passed by – Fergus curled up in bed, Fergus reading in front of the fire, Fergus having a pint in a pub, Fergus dandling a ginger-haired child on his knee. She saw him walking down a bustling London street and entering a tall building with a sign that read *The Times*. 'Fleet Street,' she said. 'That's where you end up.'

'I'm going to be famous, aye?'

'I promise.'

He let go of her hand. 'Lord knows I'd like to believe

that. But how do I know you're not just telling me what I want to hear?'

Lizzie leaned close and whispered in his ear: 'Because I saw that late at night, when you're all alone in bed, you suck your thumb.'

Fergus's eyes widened in surprise.

Lizzie sat back and folded her arms, satisfied. 'So, are you going to give Fitzy's Circus a good write-up, then?'

Fergus grinned, snatched up his hat and bowed as he left the tent. 'Surely you must know the answer to that already … fortune-teller.'

After putting away her crystal ball and taking off her robes, Lizzie came out of her tent and heard an odd noise. It sounded like someone taking long, snuffling breaths.

'Hello?' she called, wondering if one of the animals had somehow escaped.

A whining noise came from behind one of the penny gaff tents. It was definitely human. Lizzie ran round behind the tent and saw a little girl sitting on the ground, her face buried in her hands.

'What's the matter, sweetheart? Are you lost?'

The child lifted her head miserably, and even

through the drizzle of tears, Lizzie recognized her at once. 'Amelia?'

'You're not the fairy lady,' Amelia stammered, and let out a bawl.

Lizzie hugged her. 'It's all right, precious. Where's Maisie? And your Uncle Ally?'

'I don't know!' wailed Amelia. 'Maisie took me to the park in Uncle Ally's carriage for a picnic and then we had a little nap on the blanket. Only I didn't fall asleep – I saw the top of the big tent across the park and walked all the way over to it. I only wanted to see my fairy again…'

CHAPTER 6

Lizzie knocked on the door of Collette's caravan.

'Is this where the fairy lives?' Amelia asked, sounding suspicious.

'Yes.'

'I thought she would live in a big mushroom.'

'Well, this one don't,' said Lizzie. 'She lives in a magic house with wheels on.'

She patted Amelia's golden-curled head, feeling sorry for her. What must it be like, to have a head so stuffed with fairy nonsense? The real world wasn't somewhere where fairies lived. The real world was factories, dirt and meanness.

'My mummy's gone to Heaven,' Amelia said.

'So's mine,' said Lizzie, and squeezed her hand. She knocked again.

Collette finally answered the door, frowning, without make-up and with papers twisted in her hair. She'd changed out of her costume and into her normal clothes and Lizzie's heart sank – Amelia wouldn't recognize her fairy in this state. But Collette's grumpy expression changed to a smile instantly when she saw Amelia.

'Hello, little one! How lovely to see you again.'

'Fairy lady!' squealed Amelia. 'You're in disguise.'

'I found her round the back of the penny gaffs,' Lizzie explained. 'Looks like she ran off from her nursemaid and got lost. I dunno what to do with her!'

'Leave this to me.' Collette swept down the caravan steps, picked Amelia up and lifted her onto her hip – Lizzie noticed her wincing slightly as she did so. 'Where I come from,' Collette said to Amelia, 'all the little fairy children love *le chocolat*. Perhaps you do too?'

'Choc'lit?' Amelia said, her eyes shining with hope.

'Off to the tea tent we shall go!' Collette sang. She danced across the grass, carrying Amelia, while Lizzie followed.

Amelia caught sight of the show tent's red and white stripes. 'Bouncing first?'

'*Bien sûr*, bouncing first,' Collette said, gamely changing direction and carrying the little girl into the show tent.

Collette's all right really, Lizzie thought. She acted like a diva at times, but deep down she had a good heart.

After Amelia had a quick bounce on the safety net, Lizzie and Collette rushed her over to the tea tent. Ma Sullivan brought over a plate piled high with buttered crumpets and a whole mug of hot chocolate. 'There. Get that down her. I'll run and tell Fitzy about our wee guest.'

'We'll keep her happy in the meantime,' Lizzie assured her.

Collette sat Amelia on her knee while the little girl drank her chocolate. 'Do you speak any French, little one?'

Amelie shook her head.

'Well, this is *la table*, and the circus is called *le cirque*. And if you need to say "fairy" in French, you say *la fée.*'

'Like Morgan le Fay!' Lizzie said.

'Very good, Lizzie.' Collette said, laughing.

Amelia put on her serious face again. 'You do believe in fairies, don't you?'

'Of course I do,' Collette answered. 'They are all around us. The fairies put the dew on the morning flowers and decorate the spiders' webs with diamonds.'

Oh, blimey, thought Lizzie. *They're all at it.* Collette was laying it on a bit thick, but she clearly did believe in fairies, just like Ma Sullivan. *Is it just me who lives in the real world? Sometimes it feels like I'm the only grown-up in this whole bloomin' circus.*

Fitzy arrived, helped himself to a crumpet and dug in his pockets for some money. 'Bringing home waifs and strays, Lizzie?' he asked with a grin. 'I thought that was Malachy's trick.' Malachy had found Lizzie sleeping in a pile of straw, and he'd persuaded Fitzy to let her join the circus.

'She's lost,' Lizzie said.

'You're the ringmaster!' Amelia slipped out of Collette's arms, ran to Fitzy and startled him with a hug around the leg. 'Can I watch your circus again?'

'Another time, little missy. Collette, you need to get ready. Show's about to start.'

'Oh, *mon Dieu!*' Collette leaped up. 'Is it that time already?'

'Afraid so. Lizzie, we need to get this little creature back to her family right away. Here's ten shillings. Go and flag down a hackney carriage.'

'But I don't know where she lives.'

'Use your noodle, dear. She's Alexander MacDonald's niece, isn't she?'

Of course, Lizzie thought. *He's one of the wealthiest men in town. Every single cab driver in Edinburgh is going to know where his house is.*

Lizzie sat on a chilly leather seat in the back of a hansom cab, which jolted and juddered as the driver hurried them towards the New Town. Fitzy's money had paid for a fast ride, not a comfortable one.

Amelia peered out of the rain-flecked window. 'Are we nearly there yet?'

'I bloomin' hope so,' Lizzie said. 'I'm rattling about like a farthing in a blind man's tin.'

The wheels crunched on gravel. Lantern light flooded in through the glass. They were turning into a broad driveway. Up ahead, they could see the turrets and high windows of an expansive Georgian house.

'Whoa there,' the driver called to his horses, reining them in. 'Easy now!' They pulled up outside the front steps and the driver gave three short knocks on the carriage roof, to tell his passengers the journey was over.

'This is my house!' Amelia yelled. She tugged Lizzie's coat sleeve. 'Come and see my nursery. You can stay if you want.'

'I dunno if your uncle would like that.' Feeling wobbly, Lizzie climbed out and paid the driver. 'Keep the change, mate. And come see Fitzy's circus.'

The driver tipped his hat. 'Will do.'

Amelia was already running across the gravel to her own front door. She jumped up, trying to reach the knocker, but wasn't tall enough. Instead, she banged on the door three times with her little fist.

The door opened instantly and warm light flooded out into the rainy courtyard. Alexander MacDonald was standing in the hallway, and Lizzie heard his cry of, 'Oh, thank God!' He fell to his knees and clasped Amelia in a huge hug.

He must have been waiting behind the door, Lizzie realized, just in case anyone knocked with news of Amelia. She approached, and his eyes met hers – there was a depth of gratitude in them that went beyond words. Then he screwed them up tight, embracing his niece again.

'Where did you go, my heart?' he said into her shoulder. 'Where'd you wander off to, eh?'

'I ran away to the circus,' Amelia said matter-of-factly.

'But why? Are you unhappy here at home with Uncle Ally?'

'Don't be silly, Uncle! I just wanted to see the fairy again.'

Someone behind MacDonald cleared his throat and stepped forward and Lizzie froze as she saw it was a police constable. She felt a strong urge to run away.

'I take it there's no further need for this missing person report, Mister Macdonald?' he said.

'No. Thank you, Constable.'

'Very good, sir. Glad to see she's safe and sound.'

The policeman glanced at Lizzie as he left the house. He hesitated on the doorstep. 'I'll be honest with you, sir. You ought to keep a closer eye on the girl. There's people out there who like to target the children of well-to-do families.'

'You mean kidnappers,' said MacDonald coldly. He hadn't relaxed his grip on Amelia.

'That's right, sir. Stop by the station some time – I'll show you some of the ransom notes we've seen, and the threats that came with them.' The policeman nodded to Lizzie. 'Obliged to you, miss. Good night, now.'

Well, that's a first, thought Lizzie. *A policeman being polite to me.*

'Come in, Miss Brown, please,' MacDonald urged her. 'Let me take your coat. Amelia, you're going straight upstairs to bed.'

Amelia planted a kiss on Lizzie's cheek and went stomping happily up the stairs, just as Maisie the nursemaid was coming down them. 'Oh, thank heavens, she's back!'

'Aye, she is,' said MacDonald, his face like thunder. 'No, don't go back up with her, Maisie. Stay here.'

Uh oh, Lizzie thought. *I bet I know what's coming. MacDonald ain't happy with her.*

Once little Amelia was out of earshot, MacDonald rounded on Maisie furiously. 'You let her go running off to the circus? Good God, woman, were you not watching her at all?'

'I only closed my eyes for a few minutes!' Maisie wailed. 'I thought she was having a nap after our picnic.'

MacDonald ran his fingers through his hair,

distraught. 'She could have been killed, or abducted, or … or…'

'But sir, she's safe and sound now.'

'Aye, no thanks to you.' MacDonald stiffened his back and pulled himself together. 'You're no' dependable, Maisie Hendry. I took a chance when I hired you, because you seemed kind and I felt sorry for you, but now I see it was a mistake. I know my niece sees you as a friend, but you're meant to be her nursemaid, not a playmate!'

Lizzie felt terrible. Maisie was being sacked in front of her eyes, and there was nothing she could do about it. *It serves her right,* she thought, *but it's still a rotten thing to happen.*

Tears welled up in Maisie's eyes. 'Please,' she begged. 'It'll never happen again, I promise.'

'You won't need to promise. You're dismissed, without notice, on the grounds of gross irresponsibility. I need you out of here by morning. And I'll no' be giving you a reference.'

Maisie clung to the banister newels like a protester outside a palace. 'Please … for mercy's sake, give me another chance. I can't go back to factory work—'

'Go upstairs and pack your things.'

'If you had a heart…'

'Now – before I call the police again!'

Howling, Maisie pushed past Lizzie and ran up the stairs. Lizzie wondered where she would go now. She hoped she had a mother or a friend to take her in. Without a reference from MacDonald, she'd find it hard to get another job in service.

MacDonald straightened his collar. 'I'm sorry you had to see that, Lizzie. Please, come in. There's tea in the parlour.'

Large, colourful paintings hung in the hallway and Lizzie stared at them as she passed. Every single one was a scene of fairies: they skipped in circles, drank from acorn cups and floated through twilight skies, trailing gossamer behind them.

'Do you like them?' MacDonald pointed out a framed sketch of a bearded man drinking tea while fairies danced on his desk. 'There's the artist. My friend and neighbour, Charles Doyle. We're both members of the Spiritualist Society of Edinburgh.'

Lizzie tried to think of something polite to say. 'They're, er, very realistic.'

'There's a reason for that. Charles Doyle has *seen* fairies – his pictures are all painted from life.'

Lizzie bit back the sarcastic reply that rose to her lips.

A portrait of a man tormented by goblins hung at the end of the hall. They tugged on his beard and walloped his head with little hammers. *What a weird thing to hang in your house*, she thought. It reminded her of her father, who would come home steaming drunk and bellow about the elephants that were jumping on his skull.

Now she thought about it, Pa had seen fairies too. Lizzie's mind flashed back to her father huddled in the corner of a filthy room, clutching his knees and shaking like a fever victim. He'd had something called delirium tremens, a sort of spell of madness brought on by lack of alcohol.

Did these paintings show the same 'little people' her father had seen? Or maybe Charles Doyle had something else wrong with his mind.

Lizzie kept her suspicions to herself as she followed MacDonald through his huge house and into the parlour. While he busied himself with the tea things already laid out for him, Lizzie decided it was time to say her piece. 'Sir, when I spoke with your sister, she had a warning for you.'

'A warning?'

'That's what she called it. She said, "Beware of the fairy."'

A coal popped in the grate and she braced herself for MacDonald's angry response. But it didn't come. Instead, he laughed it off.

'Ach, you probably misheard. Flora loved fairies, just as much as I do. Many of those paintings you saw belonged to her.'

'But she said "beware"!'

MacDonald passed her a hot cup of tea that smelled of bergamot. Lizzie took it gingerly, afraid the delicate china would snap in her hands – she always felt ill at ease in posh people's houses, not that she'd been in many.

'She was probably reminding us to be *aware* of fairies,' he said. 'They are all around us, you know.' He held up a finger, perhaps thinking a fairy would come and perch there.

Lizzie sat in silence, sipping her tea, not knowing what to say. Nothing was going to put a dent in MacDonald's beliefs, that much was clear.

'You're sceptical?' he said at last. 'I'm surprised. A spiritually-minded person like you, not believing in fairies?'

'I don't mean no disrespect,' she said. 'I believe in spirits, because I've seen 'em and spoken to 'em. But I've never seen a fairy. They're just in stories.'

MacDonald pondered that for a moment, then fished some pieces of pink card with fancy edging out of his pocket and passed them over.

'*The Bearer is Granted Admission to a Grand Fairy Hunt,*' Lizzie read aloud, '*hosted by the Spiritualist Society of Edinburgh. Picnic included.*'

'Invitations for you and all your friends,' said MacDonald. 'I will pay their train fares as well.'

Lizzie saw the date was tomorrow. 'It's very kind of you,' she said. Should she accept? Her friends loved travelling by train and the picnic sounded delicious. It would be rude not to…

'It's the least I can do!' insisted MacDonald. 'You brought Amelia home safely.'

'You want to bring me on a fairy hunt when I don't believe in fairies?'

'Tomorrow you will see irrefutable evidence that they exist. I trust that will change your mind.'

Lizzie had a sudden vision of Amelia running through the trees, excited and heedless of danger. MacDonald must be planning to bring her on the fairy hunt too. *Beware of the fairy*, her mother's spirit had said. Not 'aware'. *Beware*. It was definitely a warning, whether MacDonald chose to heed it or not. Amelia had already got lost once by running off after a 'fairy'. This trip sounded totally ridiculous, but Lizzie couldn't take any chances when it came to the safety of a small child. She decided that Flora knew best, and she herself would be wary of fairies, even if MacDonald wouldn't.

'I'll be glad to come,' she said politely. *Even if I'm only going to keep an eye on your niece*, she thought. *My visions have never been wrong yet.*

As Lizzie left the house, she glanced up and saw Amelia waving to her from her nursery window.

'Sleep tight,' she whispered, waving back. 'And be safe.'

CHAPTER 7

To Lizzie's delight, the whole Penny Gaff Gang agreed to come with her on the fairy hunt. Collette insisted on going along too.

'At least Amelia will see her fairy, even if none of the others do,' she said.

'Are you sure you're up to it?' said Lizzie. 'I mean, your back…'

Collette shrugged. '*C'est rien*. I am used to the pain, and I love *les petites*.' She sighed dramatically. 'I want to have children of my own one day – it is good to get the practice.'

'"There is such a thing as *too* much practice,"' Erin

said, mocking Fitzy's voice, and they all laughed.

Now they all stood together on a platform at Waverley station, which lay in a valley between busy shopping streets. Lizzie wished she'd brought a scarf, because the morning was grey and gloomy – not the kind of weather for a picnic at all. *Maybe the fairies will blow the clouds away with their flapping wings*, she thought sourly.

She looked around at her friends, wishing they could afford to dress more smartly. In the circus, the children's best clothes were the ones they performed in. No expense was spared there: sequins and satin, cloth of gold and taffeta were all used. But for everyday life, they tended to wear hand-me-down clothes, darned and patched many times over.

Malachy wore a heavy overcoat, Nora and Erin simple long dresses of black cotton with white collars, Hari britches and a shirt a size too big, and Dru his smart travelling coat over tight trousers and a rather disreputable-looking ruffled shirt. Only Collette, with her wide hat and fashionable white dress, looked respectable by Edinburgh standards. *Everyone's going to be starin' at us…*

'Look at that crowd!' someone said behind her.

'What a weird-lookin' bunch.'

Lizzie's heart sank – until she realized the man wasn't talking about them. She turned around and saw what could only be the local chapter of the Spiritualist Society, dressed for a day out hunting fairies.

An old man with white whiskers, dressed in a kilt and an explorer's pith helmet, was marching down the platform with a butterfly net over his shoulder. Behind him came two hollow-cheeked ladies – identical twins – dressed from head to toe in black, followed by a fat gentleman with a box hanging around his neck from a leather strap. Lizzie wondered what was in the box. Next came a thin young man in tweed wearing goggles with purple lenses, looking around himself excitedly and making notes in a book.

'What on earth?' murmured Hari.

'I'm having second thoughts about this!' Nora said. Beside her, Erin was snorting giggles through her nose.

To Lizzie's relief, the rest of the Spiritualist crowd descending the stairs looked a lot more normal. She saw Alexander MacDonald, who waved. Behind him came Douglas Grant, surrounded by a crowd of female admirers. *Uh oh*, she thought.

'There must be about twenty people here,' Malachy

said. 'That's a lot of oddballs.'

'Be polite!' Lizzie nudged him. 'We're their guests. And they're feeding us, remember?'

Malachy pulled out a pocketwatch. 'Half an hour there, half an hour back, most of the day spent chasing after fairies … I don't see how we're going to get back to Holyrood Park for six.'

'We will.'

'We'd better. We can't miss tonight's show or Dad'll string us up.'

'Mr MacDonald promised we'd be back in plenty of time,' Lizzie assured him. 'There he is. Good morning, sir. Good morning, Amelia.'

'Lizzie!' squealed Amelia. Behind her a man with thin, grizzled hair and a bushy beard winced and clutched his head at the noise. Lizzie recognized him from the portrait in MacDonald's house – the one in which he was being tormented by goblins. It was the painter, Charles Doyle.

'Can you please lower your voice, Amelia?' the man begged. 'My head is throbbing this morning.'

He's got a hangover, Lizzie thought. *Pa used to get those.*

'Ah, introductions,' said MacDonald. 'Lizzie, permit

me to present Mr Charles Doyle. He has a gift for seeing the fairies.'

'Charmed,' Doyle said, blinking as if he were only just waking up. He offered Lizzie a sweaty hand to shake, as if she was a gentleman. She dropped a curtsey instead. Doyle realized his mistake and ran a hand through his thinning hair. His eyes wobbled unsteadily in his head, reminding Lizzie of an old toy whose pieces were falling apart.

'And this,' said MacDonald, 'is his son.'

A teenaged boy stepped forward. 'Arthur Conan Doyle,' he said with relish, as if his own name tasted good on his tongue. 'Capital to meet you. Lizzie Brown, eh? I've heard of you, I think.'

'You might've,' Lizzie said, grinning. She liked Arthur immediately. He wasn't exactly handsome, with his struggling moustache and gangly walk, but he had a rich voice that she wanted to sit down and listen to.

Arthur snapped his fingers. 'I've got it. The Phantom! You unmasked him, didn't you? Down in London.'

'Lizzie and her gang solve lots of mysteries,' Malachy said. He paused and added 'That's us: the Penny Gaff Gang.'

'I can see I'll have to get to know you all as soon

as possible,' Arthur laughed. 'I want to know all your secrets. Mysteries! How do you get to the bottom of them, eh?'

'I'm psychic,' Lizzie said with pride.

'A psychic detective.' Arthur tapped his nose. 'What an idea. I may steal it for one of my stories.'

'You must forgive Arthur,' MacDonald laughed. 'He fancies himself a writer, and he's always writing his friends into his stories.'

Charles Doyle tugged at his son's sleeve and jerked his head at an approaching throng of people. 'Beware, Arthur!' he hissed. 'Dionysus and his maenads are coming!'

Lizzie looked blank.

'He means I should hide,' Arthur said with an apologetic look, 'because Douglas Grant and his crowd of women are heading my way.'

Lizzie felt a cold lurch in her stomach – she and Grant hadn't exactly hit it off. As he strode down the station platform as if he owned it, a group of five or six Spiritualist women of varying ages surrounded him. They were saying things like, 'Oh, pay it no mind' and, 'It's just the spite of lesser creatures, dear'.

'They're fawning on him,' Erin said, grimacing.

'It's disgusting, so it is.'

It wasn't just that, Lizzie saw. They were *reassuring* him. But why?

Grant saw her. Their eyes locked for a moment, and his narrowed. Then he stopped, and the crowd of women stopped with him. They all glared at Lizzie, coming no closer.

Grant muttered something Lizzie couldn't make out, but she caught the word 'libel'. The women around him nodded like hens pecking up corn.

'What's his problem?' Lizzie wondered aloud.

Malachy pointed back up the platform to where to a newspaper-seller was waving the latest edition of the *Edinburgh Gazette*. 'Um, I think that might be the reason.'

The headline announced: FAMOUS MEDIUM A FAKE!

'Oh, blimey,' Lizzie said. 'Fergus. He did it.'

'Come on,' Nora urged. 'Everyone's getting on the train. We need to find seats.'

'Wait a moment!' Malachy went hobbling back down the platform as fast as he could. Lizzie looked from him to the train, and back, then with a gasp of frustration, she followed the others onto the train.

The others sat down, but Lizzie waited by the door to the carriage. The guard scowled at her. 'All aboard now, please!' he yelled.

'Hurry up, Mal!' Lizzie called to him.

Malachy, who had bought a newspaper, came hurrying back down the platform. All the train doors had slammed shut. Lizzie swore and flung hers back open. The guard shouted something at her but she paid him no heed as she held her hand out to her friend.

Seconds later, she grabbed Malachy's hand and pulled him onto the train.

'Sorry,' he gasped as the red-faced guard slammed their door and blew his whistle. 'But we can't miss this. Scoop of the century.'

He sat back in his seat like a businessman and unfolded the paper. The rest of the Penny Gaff Gang huddled around to listen.

'The ancient Egyptians were bamboozled by their priests,' he read, 'being led to believe that a hollow statue of Memnon was speaking. It seems the tradition of fooling the faithful is alive and well today. We have gone behind the scenes and EXPOSED the stage trickery of one of the world's most eminent mediums, the darling of America, Mr Douglas Grant himself.

Every one of his famous set pieces, including the levitation for which he is so renowned, is nothing more than FAKERY, and this paper will not stand for it.'

Lizzie felt giddy and a little bit sick. The rocking, rattling train didn't help, so she tugged the window open for some fresh air.

As Malachy read on, Lizzie recognized everything she and her friends had told Fergus. The phosphorus oil to make his hands glow, the painted bar on which Grant stood to levitate, the cold-reading techniques … it was all in there. Fergus had gone for the jugular, like a fighting terrier.

Malachy shook his head and whistled. 'Almost makes you feel sorry for Grant, this. He's ruined now. Down for the count.'

'I ain't so sure about that,' Lizzie muttered. Grant had already tried to have her thrown in the river. Now the stakes were raised, and there was no telling how he'd seek revenge for this.

She squirmed in her seat when Malachy reached the end of the article: 'Compared with Mr Grant's elaborate stage show, Miss Lizzie Brown's small tent appears humble. There is no flash and dazzle here, no patter, no stagecraft. There is only the plain light of simple truth. Have we not learned, time and again, that the Spirit appears not amidst wealth and glory, but among humble things? Did not Our Lord enter the world in a manger, between an ox and an ass?'

'Strewth,' Lizzie said.

Malachy raised his eyebrows. 'Customers should not be deceived. There is but one genuine psychic in Edinburgh, and that is Lizzie Brown of Fitzy's Travelling Circus.' He folded the paper away.

'No wonder Grant was looking daggers at you!' Nora burst out. 'You'll be neck-deep in customers after this.'

'Serves him right,' Erin said. 'Pompous ass. This'll take him down a peg.'

Lizzie thought uneasily of the day ahead. Grant would be there, along with all his devoted followers, and it was sure to be awkward. 'Maybe we shouldn't have come.'

'But it will be fun!' Dru said. He gave Lizzie a look she knew all too well. The twinkly-eyed boy had mischief in mind.

* * *

The train rattled on, passing out of Edinburgh and through green hilly land that Lizzie thought was beautiful. She could understand people believing in fairies if they'd grown up in a country like this. Old flint stone walls, ancient cottages with smoking chimneys ... there must have been stories told around those firesides for centuries, passed down from mother to daughter, generation to generation.

Amelia came bounding in to their compartment and settled herself on Collette's lap. 'I'm bored,' she announced.

'We can't have that,' Collette laughed.

'Everyone in my carriage is talking about boring grown-up stuff. So I've come to talk to you instead.'

Lizzie still had stories on her mind. 'Maybe Erin or Nora can tell you a fairy story?'

'Oh, we can!' Nora said.

'We could keep you in stories all the way to Land's End,' Erin added.

Amelia snuggled between the twins while they told her the tale of the giant Finn McCool, and how he'd tricked the bigger, more fearsome giant, Cuchulain. 'When Finn heard that Cuchulain was coming to fight him, he asked his wife to disguise him as a baby!' Erin explained.

Lizzie had heard the story from Ma Sullivan a dozen times already. Nora and Erin made a brilliant double act, with Nora telling the story and Erin doing the voices. *It's a shame there are no little children in our circus*, she thought, *because those two would be the best big sisters ever.*

'Cuchulain crashed in through the door,' said Nora.

'"I've come to fight Finn!"' Erin bellowed. '"Where is the coward?"'

'So Finn's wife pointed to the *enormous* cradle where Finn lay. "Finn's not home, but there's our baby son."'

'"Thunder and blazes! If that's the size of the baby, then how big must the father be?"'

Amelia fidgeted excitedly all through the story and clapped when it was finished. 'I love fairy stories,' she said. 'Maisie used to read them to me.' Her happy smile suddenly vanished. 'Maisie had to leave.'

'I'm so sorry,' Lizzie said.

'But I'll see her again,' Amelia said. 'I know I will.'

Lizzie didn't have the heart to tell the little girl that she'd probably never see her nanny again.

Amelia suddenly lunged out of her seat and jumped up at the window and Lizzie felt a brief moment of panic before Amelia shouted, 'It's our mill! Look, everyone! There's the clock tower.'

The MacDonald woollen mill was not pretty: it was a stone-grey ogre, a monstrous thing like a giant from one of Erin and Nora's stories. Tall chimneys smoked above rows of rooftops, miserable as a prison. Lizzie couldn't see through the murky windows, but she could guess what was inside – row upon row of machines, roaring and thrumming and clattering, and people bent over them like exhausted slaves. Factories ate human beings alive.

Amelia, though, was beaming with pride. To her, it was a family treasure.

'You all right, Lizzie?' Nora asked. 'You've gone all quiet.'

Lizzie was remembering another factory, and the stink of phosphorus oil clouded her mind. She saw the ragged children coughing, the women with rotting, infected jaws bound up with bandage. Phossy jaw, it was called.

'Lizzie? What's wrong?' Erin was concerned as well.

Lizzie shuddered. 'I don't like factories,' she said. 'My brother died from working in one – I can't stand to look at them now.'

'Maisie didn't like factories either,' Amelia said. 'She said they hurt children. But our mill is nice.'

'Have you ever been inside?'

'Course I haven't, silly. But it makes such pretty things.' Amelia smoothed the fine woollen fabric of her skirt.

At what cost? Lizzie thought darkly, and glanced back at the mill windows.

It was a relief when, not too far beyond the mill, the train finally stopped. Everyone piled out of the carriages and onto the country station platform. Three groups quickly formed: the Penny Gaff Gang and Amelia, Grant and his hangers-on, and MacDonald and the eccentrics, including the Doyles.

'This way,' MacDonald called, and swung a gate open onto a path.

Lizzie saw Grant was glaring at her again. She turned away with her nose in the air. She was here now, and she might as well try to enjoy it, even if Grant was doing his best to make her feel unwelcome.

The path led up into a pine wood. For Lizzie, who had only ever seen forests from the top of a moving caravan, it looked like a shadowy and bewitching labyrinth. Huge trunks loomed out of the mist and a sweet scent of pine reached her nose.

'It's beautiful,' she said to herself.

The pine trees were as tall as the factory chimneys, but they were green and bursting with life, and the air was pure and clean. As they moved from the bright sunshine into the welcoming woods, where shafts of light slanted cathedral-like from between the branches, Lizzie felt a tingle of excitement.

In a place like this, untouched by man since the dawn of time, perhaps fairies really could exist...

CHAPTER 8

'So, Mr MacDonald, what do we actually *do* on a fairy hunt?' Lizzie asked, as they walked along the wooded path.

'We walk, we remember the lore, and we keep our eyes – and our minds – open.' MacDonald helped Lizzie to leap over a tiny stream, dappled with mossy green stones like the heads of submerged creatures. 'These woods are sacred. There are legends of the Little People going back centuries.'

'What sorts of legends?' Lizzie wanted to know.

'Where should I begin?' MacDonald carried a cane, like many gentlemen, and he used it to point out a ring of spotted toadstools. 'Fairies aren't just the pretty wee creatures dancing around toadstools in nursery books. There's many kinds – boggarts, goblins, selkies, the Seelie and the Unseelie Courts. Legend has it that this very wood is Caterhaugh, where young Janet saved her love Tam Lin from the faerie queen.'

'I know that tale!' Erin said. 'The queen took Tam Lin for herself, but Janet rescued him. The fairies turned him into all sorts of beasts, but she held on tight to him, no matter how hideous he became, until he turned back into a man.'

'Ain't fairies meant to be nice?' Lizzie said, a little alarmed.

'Fairies are nature spirits, and nature must be treated with respect,' warned MacDonald. 'They are the beauty of the rose, but also the sharpness of the thorn.'

They were deep in the woods now. The branches overhead let in only a struggling light and the path was little more than a faint trail, buried under pine needles and spongy moss. Lizzie was still excited, and scolded herself for it. *Stop getting worked up*, she told herself. *There's nothing here.*

'Stop!' Hari whispered urgently, only feet away. 'There!' He pointed.

Startled, Lizzie turned to look. Hari couldn't have seen a fairy, could he?

At first she saw nothing. Then, slowly, a head lifted itself into view and Lizzie saw deep dark eyes and curved antlers, rising up like a crown of power.

It was a stag – a beautiful, royal stag – watching them through the branches. Lizzie stood transfixed, caught up in the moment, until a twig snapped nearby. Startled, the stag dashed away, bounding between the trees and vanishing from sight.

She grabbed Hari's arm and they grinned at each other. 'I saw it!' she said. 'That was amazing!'

'Glad you came?' Hari said. 'Here, look at this heather. It's supposed to be lucky.'

Lizzie wasn't really listening. She was still thinking of the stag's hypnotic dark eyes that seemed to see straight into her very soul. Next thing she knew, Dru's long fingers were touching her head. He tucked something behind her ear quickly. 'Oi!' she yelled and jumped away from him. 'What are you playing at?'

He held up the rest of a bunch of purple Michaelmas daisies he'd picked. 'It suits you, having flowers in your hair,' he smiled. 'You look like a fairy queen.'

Lizzie reached up, thinking she'd pull them out and

fling them away, but then hesitated and changed her mind. 'I'm a bit young to be a queen, ain't I?'

'Beauty is timeless,' Dru said with a grin.

That was too much. Lizzie strode on ahead of him to where Arthur Conan Doyle and his father were making their way up the side of a grassy green mound. More sunlight filtered through in this part of the wood – it felt a bit like being under limelight at the circus.

'Whoops!' Charles Doyle said, as his unsteady legs gave way beneath him. Arthur caught his arm quickly and helped him back up. Lizzie helpfully took his other arm, then wished she hadn't, for Charles Doyle's breath reeked of alcohol.

'Watch your step, Father,' Arthur said, with an apologetic glance at Lizzie. 'The Little People are tricksy.'

'Ha! Troublesome little fellows, tripping me up!' Doyle wagged a finger at the branches and shadows around him. 'You won't catch me out with your fairy tricks.'

Amelia chose that moment to run up behind him and shout 'Boo!' Doyle nearly went toppling over again. Amelia giggled and ran off behind a tree, shouting, 'You can't find me!'

'Do be careful, Amelia,' MacDonald sighed, chasing after her, and Lizzie flashed back to her vision of MacDonald running after his sister – she smiled to think what Flora would make of such a wild little girl, growing up in her own image.

She reached the top of the hill and stood there with Hari, Arthur and Charles Doyle. High in the trees, birds chirped and chittered. For the first time, it struck her as odd that a little hill should be here like this, rising up from the forest floor like a bowler hat under a green blanket. It didn't seem to fit.

'What is this place?' she asked.

'A fairy mound,' Arthur said. 'They mark the entrances into the Otherworld. In Ireland, the Good Folk are called the *sidhe*. It means the people of the mounds.'

'It's also a tomb,' his father said. 'They buried people in mounds like this, thousands of years ago.'

'Really?' Lizzie gasped.

Arthur nodded. 'Sometimes you find gold and silver in them. And skeletons, of course.'

Lizzie looked down, thinking about old brown bones in the earth beneath her feet, and golden bangles around them. A pretty pinecone caught her eye.

It wasn't gold, but it was a treasure. She picked it up.

'Stop!' Nora shouted. She ran up the hill with Erin close behind. 'Don't!'

'What?'

'You took something!' Erin said. The anger in her face made Lizzie step back.

'It's only a pinecone, see?' She held it up.

Nora tutted in annoyance. 'Why won't you listen, Lizzie? Never, ever take anything from the fairies, or they'll be angry with you!'

Lizzie rolled her eyes and shoved it into her pocket anyway.

A little further ahead, MacDonald pointed out a bulge of rock that broke the surface of the forest floor like a sea monster's hump. 'Now you'll see something to make you a believer, my young sceptic,' he said to Lizzie.

'It's a rock,' Lizzie said, unimpressed. 'Or maybe this lot think it's a troll in disguise.'

Grant flashed her an angry look at that.

'Look closer,' said MacDonald. 'There, under that patch of moss. Do you see?'

The rock was covered with strange markings, the same pattern repeated over and over: a deep depression, with a shallower ring around it. 'Cup and ring markings,' Arthur announced solemnly. 'Here since long before our ancestors ever walked the land.'

Lizzie peered at them in bafflement. Like a message written in a forgotten code, they seemed to mean something, but there was no clue what it could be. The silent stone held its secrets close, and would probably hold them for centuries to come.

'I wonder who made them?' she said.

'The fairies, of course,' said an elderly woman Spiritualist. 'These are the fairies' table settings.'

'You're having a laugh!' Lizzie protested.

'Lizz-*ie!*' Nora said through gritted teeth. 'Why'd you have to be so ... augh!' She kicked up a pile of leaves, too cross to say any more.

'Why indeed?' snarled Grant. 'I trust our Doubting Thomasina is familiar with the practice of leaving out milk for the fairies?'

'Well, yes.' Lizzie did know, because Ma Sullivan did it.

The famous psychic put his finger very carefully into one of the cup markings. 'This is where offerings of milk would have been left,' he said, in a voice so soft he could have been speaking in church. 'Our ancestors were wiser than we.' The Spiritualists behind him nodded vigorously.

Lizzie gave up. She wandered back to Malachy, her hands in her pockets. 'You're smart, Mal, and not superstitious like this lot. What do you make of those markings?'

'Prehistoric people carved them, I reckon,' said Malachy. 'Couldn't tell you why. Might be a board for a Stone Age game, for all I know.'

MacDonald clapped briskly like a schoolteacher. 'Quiet, now! Can I have your attention, please? It is time for the ceremony.'

'Ceremony?' Lizzie felt the colour drain from her face. The Spiritualists gathered around the cup-and-ring stone, joining hands with one another and forming a partial circle. Nora, Erin and Collette went to join them, Collette taking Amelia's hand. Hari, Dru, Malachy and Lizzie stayed off to one side, forming a little huddle.

MacDonald called across 'No spectators, please. The ceremony is part of the day's activities.'

'Didn't ruddy say so on the invitation,' Lizzie muttered. 'What are we going to do?'

'It's join in or walk home,' Hari said, sighing.

Reluctantly they went to join the ring. Holding hands with Malachy on one side and Hari on the other, Lizzie felt supremely ridiculous. All the adults had solemn faces, as if they were taking part in something important. *This must be a dream,* Lizzie thought. In real life, normal people don't go skipping about in circles.

'I will lead the singing,' said Grant. 'Please join in or remain respectfully silent. Let our song reach into the Otherworld, and call the fairy folk to join us. We may be blessed with a manifestation.'

'A what?' Lizzie whispered.

'A fairy turning up,' Malachy whispered back.

Grant said, 'Miss Macklemore – the bell, if you please.'

One of the old ladies took a tiny silver bell out of her bag and jingled it. And all the Spiritualists began to hum.

Lizzie almost burst out laughing and barely choked it back in time. *Oh Gawd, I can't do this.* She stared at her feet, knowing she couldn't look at the Spiritualists or laughter would explode out of her and not stop.

'O fairies wonderful and true,' sang Grant in a strained baritone. 'Shining with a light of purest blue, come leave your pleasant realm and join us, do.'

'O fairies true,' chimed the Spiritualists. 'Join us, do.'

Lizzie thought about kippers. She thought about lumps of coal and muddy boots and the smell of gas. She frantically thought of all the saddest, most boring things she could. *A puppy with only three legs.* If she didn't, she was done for. Her mouth twitched. *Toast falling butter-side down.*

The circle of people began to move. They were dancing, clockwise, in a ring, singing the ridiculous song over and over again. *Ring-a-ring-a-roses*, Lizzie thought before she could stop herself, and a little strangled noise, not quite a laugh, escaped from her nose.

The dance sped up. The Spiritualists sang heartily, some of them shutting their eyes as if they were praying. Lizzie suddenly noticed that Dru was singing along with them. He was crossing his eyes and smirking as he boomed out, '…with a light of purest *blooo*!'

That did it. Lizzie's face crumpled and a glorious, shameless laugh burst out of her – she simply couldn't help it. Dru laughed too, and then Amelia, then Collette. The more the Spiritualists glared poisonously at them, the more they all laughed.

It was like the Emperor's New Clothes. Suddenly everyone could see how preposterous the whole charade was. The Spiritualists kept on singing, trying to be serious, but the spell was well and truly broken.

'Enough!' Grant shouted. 'There will be no manifestation today, and we all know where to lay the blame!' All around the circle, people released each other's hands.

'It ain't our fault,' Lizzie gasped, still laughing. 'That bloomin' song…'

'This is what happens when you bring a pack of circus children on a serious spiritual outing,' Grant fumed.

As Grant's crowd stormed off, Amelia surprised MacDonald with a hug. 'That was so funny! I bet the fairies laughed too.'

'I'm sure they did,' Charles Doyle said, still laughing.

The chosen picnic site was a clearing in the forest. Lizzie sat down on a log and watched wind-blown seeds dancing through the golden sunbeams. *It must be after midday now*, she thought, but with nature all around her, she was losing track of time. She was used to the heartbeat of the city, not this wild outdoor space.

The party spread out tartan picnic blankets and unpacked the hampers. Grant's bunch of Spiritualists were giving the circus children a wide berth now, setting out their feast on the opposite side of the clearing. Lizzie didn't mind a bit.

While the Spiritualists chatted about the different types of fairies, from the evil Jenny Greenteeth to the helpful Cauld Lad of Hilton, Dru brought Lizzie a plateful of Scottish delicacies to try. 'Smoked salmon,' he said. 'Oatcakes and *fromage*. Bottled lemonade! We are living the high life now, eh?'

'This is more like it,' Lizzie agreed, tucking in. Fairies might not be real, but this feast was, and it made the whole trip worth it. Amelia smiled across at her, her face covered in shortbread crumbs.

Later, as everyone sat relaxing and the plates were packed away, Douglas Grant stood up and sauntered to the centre of the clearing. *Uh-oh*, Lizzie thought. *He's up to something.*

'To round off this excellent meal,' he said, 'perhaps the famous Lizzie Brown could give us a demonstration of her psychic skills? We've all read about them in the newspaper this morning, but as they say, you can't believe everything you read. I, for one, would like to see a little proof.'

'I'm not a *performer* like you, mate,' Lizzie said coldly, without getting up. 'I only do private readings.'

His angry scowl told her she'd scored a point. 'Of course,' he retorted, 'it stands to reason you'd be afraid to have an audience. In the privacy of a dark tent, you can get up to all sorts of trickery, can't you?'

'I don't trick anybody!'

'I suppose the Lobster Boy and the Mermaid in your little freak show are real too?' Grant smirked. 'A sucker is born every minute. That's the circus proverb, isn't it?'

'You're the fraud, not me!' Lizzie yelled. 'You don't need to be a psychic to see that. You're just jealous of someone who's got real psychic powers, like you only pretend to have!'

Grant froze on the spot. He made a gurgling noise in his throat and his body shuddered.

'She's bewitched him!' one of the Spiritualist ladies screamed.

'Going … into … trance,' Grant spluttered. 'I see … the future.'

'Everybody, hush!' shouted another Spiritualist.

'Mister Grant is speaking a prophecy!'

Lizzie folded her arms and rolled her eyes. 'Here we go.'

Grant pointed at Lizzie with a shaking finger. 'Hear ye the words. Terrible misfortune shall befall you! From the gutter you came, and to the gutter you shall return!'

Biting back a rude reply, Lizzie abruptly stood up. 'Excuse me, everyone. I think I'll go for a little walk.' Her friends rose to follow her, but Lizzie shook her head. 'It's all right. I'd rather be on my own for a while.'

She walked away from the circle, heading for the shelter of the woods. Anger boiled inside her. She knew she shouldn't have risen to Grant's taunts – she had just made him look like he was right.

A scampering noise came from behind her. 'Wait for me, Lizzie!'

'Amelia? Go back to the picnic, love.'

'I want to keep looking for fairies,' Amelia said. 'Wiv you.' She took Lizzie's hand before she could say no.

Lizzie sighed. She couldn't bring herself to send the little girl away.

As they walked along hand in hand, Amelia chattered away like a little bird. 'These woods are my most favourite place,' she said. 'Me and Maisie come here for walks all the time in the summer. She says fresh air is very 'portant for wee girls.'

'Yes, it is,' Lizzie murmured. She suddenly thought of the factory they'd passed on their train journey. It wasn't far from the woods, but she'd be very surprised if the children who worked there ever got to go for woodland picnics.

'There's a special tree near here. The biggest oak tree you ever saw! Me and Maisie used to have our picnics under there,' Amelia babbled. 'I miss her. When will she come back?'

'She had to go away,' Lizzie said carefully.

'*You* can play with me. Let's play hide and seek!' yelled Amelia. 'Come on!'

'All right, then,' Lizzie said with a laugh. It would distract the little girl from asking difficult questions.

'Close your eyes as tight as you can and count to twenty!' Amelia told her.

So Lizzie did just that. She heard the drumming of footsteps and a giggle as Amelia ran away to hide. 'One, two, three…' she counted.

Wind rustled the branches overhead. A crow's harsh call rang out.

'…eleven, twelve, thirteen…'

Gooseflesh rose on Lizzie's arms. It was cold all of a sudden. She wondered if she should peep, so she could see where Amelia was going and cut the game short, but decided not to.

'…seventeen, eighteen…'

A flurry of wings made her start as some birds nearby took to the air. In the distance she heard the Spiritualists singing again.

'Twenty!' she shouted. 'Coming!'

She opened her eyes and looked around, and a slow feeling of unease crept up inside her chest – Amelia was nowhere in sight.

She checked the obvious places first, looking behind every tree and every shrub. There was no sign of the girl. She wasn't up in the branches, either. Lizzie smiled when she spotted a humped rock large enough for a child to hide behind, but there was nothing behind it save mud and leaves.

'You're very good at hiding, Amelia,' she called nervously.

No answer came.

Something caught her eye on the ground: a twist of bright blue. She picked it up – it was one of Amelia's hair ribbons.

Dread flooded her. 'Amelia, I give up! You can come out now!'

There was still no answer. Lizzie called Amelia's name again and again, but the only sound was the chirping of birds and the rustling of wind-blown leaves.

Lizzie clutched the ribbon in her fist. 'Amelia, this ain't funny. You're scarin' me. Please, *please* come out!'

No reply.

That was when she knew Amelia was gone.

CHAPTER 9

Lizzie ran blindly through the woods, stumbling through underbrush and tripping over tree roots. Branches whacked her and twigs caught in her hair, and there was no sign of the path – she no longer had any idea where she was.

'Amelia!' she yelled. 'Where are you?'

Sinister whispers seemed to come from all around as the wind stirred the leaves. Lizzie wasn't used to the woodland noises, and they made her heart pound with fear. She'd grown up with the sounds of a city – the shrieks of washerwomen, fights breaking out in back alleys, the smash and tinkle of shattered glass.

Now unseen things all around her were chittering, squawking and scratching their claws on the tree bark.

She thought of the fairy pictures Charles Doyle had drawn. She remembered skinny little figures with narrow eyes and grins too big for a human mouth. That pinecone she'd picked up was still in her pocket, and she wished she'd thrown it away now.

Beware of the fairy, Flora had warned. Had this been what she really meant? To stay away from the fairy hunt? Lizzie didn't want to believe it. If her powers had already tried to help and she'd thrown that one chance away, she might never get another…

A beating of heavy wings came from right behind her. She spun around and a shadow fell across her face. She screamed, high and shrill.

Next moment the thing was winging away again, with a rabbit clutched in its claws. Lizzie watched the dark body vanishing up through the trees. Whatever it was, it was big. An eagle? She suddenly thought with horror that there might be other creatures lurking in these woods – dangerous animals that might prey on a five-year-old girl.

Moments later, Alexander MacDonald came running out of the woods towards her, with

Arthur Conan Doyle and his father close behind. 'Lizzie? What's wrong? We heard you screaming … where's Amelia?'

'I don't know!' Lizzie howled, close to tears. 'She wanted to play hide and seek, but I can't find her anywhere!'

The look of fury on MacDonald's face made Lizzie want to run and hide. It only lasted for a second before he regained his composure. 'Amelia?' he bellowed. 'Come out from wherever you're hiding, this instant!'

Lizzie prayed the little girl would come running, muddy and dishevelled, laughing at how she'd fooled everyone. But the seconds ticked past, and nothing happened.

MacDonald became brisk. 'She's lost. We must take action. Miss Brown, take me to the last place you saw my niece. Arthur, Charles, go back to the group and tell everyone to look for her.'

'Yes, *sah*!' said Charles, with a stiff salute.

'She told me about an oak tree,' Lizzie told MacDonald as they strode between the trees. 'She used to have picnics there, she said.'

'I know the place. Come on!' MacDonald broke into a run. Lizzie sprinted after him, gasping for breath.

Fresh hope gave her strength. Through the trees, she could see the rest of the fairy hunt guests searching for Amelia.

We've got to find her, she thought. If only her powers would help! Why couldn't she just have a vision and *see* where the little girl was?

They arrived at the oak tree. As wide round as a castle tower, it loomed among the other trees like a king. No wonder Amelia had loved it so much. But as they searched around the huge trunk, there was no sign of her.

'She's not here,' MacDonald said. He staggered to a halt and stood looking around in bewilderment. 'I thought … I was sure…'

The other searchers emerged into the clearing to join them. 'No sign,' Arthur said, wiping his forehead.

'The sun's going to go down soon,' said Malachy.

'He's right,' said Arthur. 'She has to be found before nightfall, or we might never find her. We need to go to the police – they can get bloodhounds on the job.'

The Spiritualist with the explorer's helmet muttered something, and the others all nodded gravely. 'I beg your pardon?' MacDonald demanded.

'I was saying the fairies probably took her,' the old

man said. 'Bloodhounds won't do any good if she's been taken to the fairy kingdom, will they?'

Lizzie wanted to slap him for that. 'A little girl's gone missing and you're still blathering about fairies?'

'You were warned!' Grant yelled, pointing an accusing finger at Lizzie. 'All along you've mocked and sneered. Well, now an innocent has had to pay the price for your arrogance.'

Lizzie stood dumbfounded. Her mouth opened and closed. *He's blaming me?*

Grant took her silence as proof of her guilt. 'We all know the fairies take human children when they are insulted. You made them angry, Lizzie Brown. The blame rests with *you*!'

The police station in the nearby town was not a cheery place. The walls were the cold, grubby white of dirty London snow. Faded posters pinned up on a board showed the ugly faces of wanted murderers, crooks and burglars.

Lizzie couldn't stop thinking of little Amelia, alone in the forest with nobody to show her the way home.

'Next,' barked a police officer. An elderly Spiritualist stood, smoothed down her gown and walked with a sigh into the back room.

Everyone who had been on the fairy hunt was crammed into the police station's waiting room. There was not enough room for everyone to sit, so the ladies took the benches while the men stood or went outside to smoke pipes. The police were taking statements from every one of them, one at a time. It was taking hours, and nobody would have recognized the happy troupe of people who had set off from the railway station that morning – Amelia's disappearance had cast a gloom over them all. Only Grant seemed to be relishing the atmosphere. His narrow eyes and tight-lipped expression seemed to say *I told you so*.

Malachy wouldn't stop looking out of the window. The sky had long since turned from grey to indigo to the deep blue-black of night. Lizzie knew what he was thinking – there was no way they'd be back in time for the performance that evening.

'Next,' the policeman said.

Lizzie's thoughts churned around and around like dirty washing in murky water. The faces of the criminals on the station wall rose up in her mind, baring their teeth, reaching out with rough, blood-stained hands.

She had to help, but she didn't know how. Why wouldn't her powers *tell* her something? What was the point of having visions if she couldn't have one when she most needed one?

'Next!' The policeman sounded angry.

Dru nudged her. 'That's you, Liz.'

Liz started to her feet. 'Coming.'

The back room was even worse than the front, a featureless cell of stone lit by a single oil lamp on a central desk. A sergeant with a haggard face and thin black hair sat writing. The pen went scritch-scratch like a rat's claws. He didn't look up.

Eventually he motioned for Lizzie to sit. She felt queasy as she sat down on the little wooden stool. *This is the silent treatment. I've heard of this. The rozzers do it to get people to talk.*

She sat patiently, reminding herself she'd done nothing wrong. The sergeant lifted his eyes to her.

'You're a gypsy, are you not?'

'No, sir.'

'No?'

'I'm with the circus, but I'm a Londoner born and bred.'

He glanced at his papers. 'Fortune-teller, it says here. But you say you're not a gypsy?'

'No, sir, I'm not. But I can't see why it would matter if I was.' She knew exactly what he was driving at, and it was making her angry. Circus people weren't the only travelling folk who had lies told about them wherever they went. A child was missing, and this policeman had already made up his mind who to blame.

'You were alone with the little girl when she disappeared,' said the sergeant. 'You say she ran off. Can you say which way she went?'

'I … I can't.'

'Eh? Come, come, girl. It's a simple enough question. Which way did she go?'

Lizzie felt tears starting from her eyes and blinked them back angrily. 'I had my eyes shut. We were playing hide and seek.'

'I see.' Scratch, scratch went the pen, no doubt writing down what a fool Lizzie was.

'We've read about you,' he said at length. 'Your escapades have made the papers twice, even up here in Edinburgh.'

From his tone, Lizzie didn't think the policeman was after an autograph. 'I try and help people,' she said.

'Pull the other one,' scoffed the sergeant. 'You can't fool a Highlander like you can those London softies. We cottoned on to you long ago.'

The other policeman leaned in. 'It's funny, isn't it, how crimes just seem to happen around you?'

'Anyone would think there was some sort of connection between Miss Brown and criminality,' mused the sergeant. 'Of course, it could just be a coincidence.'

'Wallopin' great coincidence, it would have to be,' said the policeman.

Lizzie shook her head. 'No, it ain't like that.' She felt guilty and afraid over Amelia, and now these two were all but accusing her of being a criminal?

All at once, something gave way inside and she couldn't hold the tears back any longer. All the angry bitter sadness welled up inside her and flooded down her cheeks. The flame of the oil lamp blurred and split in her vision, and she sat with her face in her hands while the two policemen went to the back of the room and talked in low voices. She caught some of what they were saying: 'Seems genuinely distressed' and 'No fathomable motive'.

She heard the door being opened. 'You can go,'

the sergeant said.

Lizzie took a moment to dry her eyes on her sleeve and take a few deep breaths. She felt wretched, and Dru would probably think she looked ugly and red-eyed from crying.

'On your way!' the sergeant insisted. 'Now!'

Lizzie hurried out of the room and back to join the others. When they saw the state of her, Erin and Nora gasped and went to give her a hug. 'They were horrible,' Lizzie mumbled into Nora's shoulder. 'They thought … they reckoned I'd done something.'

'Obvious conclusion to draw,' Grant said smugly.

Nora held Lizzie tight. Slowly and deliberately, speaking so the whole room could hear, she said without drawing breath, 'Mister Grant, you're making mighty free with that mouth of yours, so you are, but you might not be aware that our Lizzie has a sizeable family backin' her up, so I'd be after shutting my mouth if I were you, or a caravan-load of Sullivan men might soon be offering to shut it for yeh, if you catch my meaning.'

Grant flinched as if every word had been a bullet. He turned pale, shuffled his feet and wisely said nothing more.

'Thanks,' Lizzie whispered to Nora.

When the police finally emerged from their back room, they told MacDonald there was nothing more they could do that day and everyone was free to go. 'We'll resume the search at dawn, sir,' the sergeant said. 'Half the town'll turn out to help, like as no'.'

'So we're just going to give up?' MacDonald looked haggard and old; he seemed to have aged twenty years in one day, like a man who'd fallen asleep in a fairy ring and woken up in the wrong century.

The sergeant was gentle but firm. 'Sir, we're working on the assumption someone's taken the wee girl. We're no' hunting for her at this stage, we're looking for evidence. If we try to do that in the dark, we could destroy vital clues.'

'You must do as you think best.' MacDonald slowly put on his hat and prepared to leave.

'Sir?'

MacDonald hesitated. 'Yes?'

'I'd keep a close eye on your mailbox for the next few days. In case—'

MacDonald nodded grimly. 'In case someone sends me a ransom demand.'

Lizzie caught a glimpse of the pain on MacDonald's

face as he left. The Penny Gaff Gang waited until all the Spiritualists had gone, then they headed out of the police station and down the hill towards the railway.

'I expect the show's over by now,' Malachy said gloomily.

Dru gave a grim laugh. 'Can't have been much of a show without the Amazing Sullivan Twins, and two of the Astonishing Boissets missing.'

Hari groaned. 'Fitzy's going to kill us.'

To Lizzie's relief, the train back to Edinburgh was mostly empty. As it pulled away, she sat at the back of the carriage they'd claimed for themselves, with the Spiritualists in a carriage of their own. MacDonald had chosen to sit with Grant and his cronies and not with her.

She looked out of the window at the woods. It would be freezing out there now. Lizzie shivered as she thought of Amelia. She might still be out there, lost, cold and alone. Or she could be somewhere even worse…

CHAPTER 10

The train eventually drew into Waverley station. Lizzie stayed glued to her seat, huddled in the darkness of their train compartment, until everyone else had left the train – she didn't want to run into MacDonald's accusing glare or Grant's sneer. Maybe it would be better if she just stayed here on the train all night, despite the freezing air that made her breath fog.

'Come on, Liz,' Malachy said, holding his hand out. 'Chin up. The police will find her, I'm sure of it.'

'I expect they will,' said Lizzie hoarsely, still looking out of the window. She didn't speak the words that whispered in her mind. *They'll find her dead, frozen under a tree, and it'll be my fault.*

'On your feet,' Malachy said. He pulled her off the train and didn't stop pulling until the Penny Gaff Gang were standing together in the street. They looked at one another, at a loss for what to do next. The thought of going back to the circus and telling Fitzy what had happened wasn't very appealing.

Collette suddenly exclaimed. '*Alors!* It's Fergus!'

The journalist was walking along the road opposite, and seemed to be deep in thought. He changed direction at once when he heard their calls, weaving through the pedestrians and horse-drawn carriages and finally running up to meet them. 'Fancy bumping into you lot at this time of night! Go on, then. What's the scoop?'

'Scoop?' Lizzie said, wondering how he could have known.

Fergus laughed. 'You're at the train station instead of at the circus. Wasn't tonight supposed to be your gala performance? There's definitely something dodgy going on – I can tell from your faces. You all look like a pack of foxes caught raiding a henhouse!' He chuckled, then saw the solemn looks they were giving back. 'Oh,' he said. 'This is bad news, isn't it?'

'Very bad,' Lizzie said.

Fergus rubbed his hands together briskly. 'Bad news is still news. If you've got a story, I want to hear it.'

'It's Amelia,' Lizzie began, but Fergus hushed her.

'No, not here in the street! Let me take you somewhere we won't be overheard…'

The steak-house Fergus took them to was rowdy, brassy and full of light. They had to push their way in through the crowd of people already waiting. Whiskery men shouted at one another across tables and Lizzie saw blood mixed in with the sawdust on the floor. *Maybe it's from the steaks*, she thought hopefully.

'What'll you have, Fergie?' hollered the woman behind the counter, who had mounds of red hair and a body like a prizefighter. Nora and Erin stared at her in awe.

'Biggest pot of tea you can make, Norma, and a round of oatcakes.'

'Back room?'

'If you please!'

Soon they were huddled together around a

table in an untidy little room piled up with broken furniture. There was even an old piano in the corner, candelabra and all. Fergus swept the picked-clean oyster shells and crumpled papers off the table with his arm. 'It's not fancy,' he admitted, 'but it's private. Now, tell me everything.'

Lizzie told the whole story while Fergus nodded gravely and made notes. It made her sick with worry to think of what the newspapers would say. Every time her name had been in the headlines before, it had been to praise her as a heroine. What would the papers say about her now?

At least Fergus was a friend. She felt she could trust him. She hoped she could, at any rate.

A huge tray of tea, oatcakes and cheeses arrived. Everyone gratefully helped themselves, except Lizzie. She couldn't stop thinking of Amelia, who'd probably had nothing to eat tonight.

'So, Miss Brown,' said Fergus. 'Where is she?'

'I ... I don't know,' Lizzie said, startled. Did he think she was behind it?

'I know you don't know,' he said evenly. 'I'm asking you for an opinion. Little girls don't just vanish into thin air. So where is she?'

'The fairies took her,' said Nora.

Lizzie groaned. 'Come off it! Not this again!'

'No, Lizzie, *you* come off it!' Erin snapped. 'All those old stories don't just come out of nothin', you know. No smoke without fire, right?'

'Fairies do make off with human children,' Nora said sadly. 'They're known for it. Amelia wouldn't be the first.'

Lizzie rolled her eyes, but that just made Erin angrier. 'God's sake, Lizzie, wake up! You're a psychic! You talk to flamin' *ghosts*! But you're a sceptic when it comes to fairies, are you? Where's the sense in that?'

Malachy came to her rescue. 'Lay off her, you two. You've said your piece.' He rapped his teaspoon on the table like a judge calling for order in court. 'Let's look for another explanation for Amelia disappearing. A *rational* one, that makes sense to all of us.'

Fergus nodded. 'What about her uncle, Alexander MacDonald? He's got the motive.'

'Of course!' Malachy said, slapping his head.

Collette looked confused. 'His own niece? Why?'

'MacDonald only owns half the woollen mill,' Fergus explained. 'The other half's in her name. If little Amelia was out of the way, it would all belong to him.'

'There's a lot of money in that mill,' Hari said. 'He'd be even richer than he is now.'

'That's horrible,' Collette shuddered.

'And it ain't true,' Lizzie exploded. 'He'd never let anything happen to her. He loves her! I've seen it for myself.'

'Greed can be a powerful motive,' Fergus said with a shrug. 'Some of the things I've seen, in this job…' His voice trailed off.

'So she's dead,' Lizzie said, her voice shaking. 'That's what you reckon, ain't it? She's been killed because her uncle wanted more money.' Dru reached to give her hand a comforting squeeze, but she jerked it away. 'And it's my fault.'

'No,' Dru insisted.

'It is. She ran off while I was playing hide and seek with her. I should have stopped her … I should—'

'Stop that, right now,' Malachy told her. 'I know you feel bad, Lizzie. We all do. But crying isn't going to bring her back, is it?'

Lizzie pulled herself together. He was right – she had no business feeling sorry for herself when Amelia might still be out there, needing her help. She took a deep, stuttering breath and let it out again. 'Thanks,

Mal. But we do need to do *something*.'

Hari spoke up. 'What do we usually do when we have a mystery to solve?'

'Most times, we start from one of Lizzie's visions,' Malachy said. 'I wonder ... Liz, could you use your powers?'

'I can't just make a vision happen. They come to me.'

'But if Amelia's dead…'

Lizzie realized what he was asking her to do. The thought horrified her, but she knew she had no choice.

'I could try and talk to her spirit,' she said reluctantly. 'But I'd have to have something that belonged to her.'

Suddenly she remembered the hair ribbon in her pocket. It had been lying there in the forest, the only trace left of Amelia, and she'd picked it up. Slowly she pulled it out and lay it on the table in front of them all.

'There's a stroke of luck,' Malachy said.

'Go on, tell us what you can see!' Fergus leaned in expectantly.

'*Mon Dieu!*' hissed Collette. 'Leave her alone. Don't you understand what you're asking? She was the last to see Amelia alive, and now you all want her to see her dead?'

They all sat back, a little shamefaced.

'Sorry, Lizzie. You don't have to.'

'Yes I do, Mal,' Lizzie said. 'I let her down back there in the woods. I ain't going to do that twice.'

She held onto the blue ribbon as if it had been Amelia's hand and tried to empty her mind of all thoughts, but they bubbled up nonetheless: *What if I don't see her?* Then, on the heels of that: *What if I do? What if the poor little thing is dead, but doesn't know it yet? I'll have to be the one to tell her…*

Images were forming behind her eyes. She took a sharp breath. It was beginning.

But Amelia's spirit didn't appear. Instead, Lizzie was seeing things through Amelia's eyes, but not as she was now. A younger Amelia was holding out her chubby arms to Flora – her mother – who laughed and picked her up.

Something was shimmering in the corner of her eye. She felt Amelia craving it, *needing* to see it. A fairy? Then, as the colourful blaze swung into view, she understood. It was a Christmas tree, covered with tiny candles and glittering ornaments. Amelia's laughter echoed in her mind.

'Help me, Amelia,' Lizzie whispered. 'Show me

what I need to see.'

More images flashed through her mind. Amelia, dressed in black, crying at her mother's funeral. Amelia looking down at a picture book, mouthing the words as she read them. Now she was jumping up and down as a kindly-looking woman poured hot water into a bath tub. Maisie? No, some other nanny. This must be from before Maisie's time.

Lizzie flew through the years of Amelia's life like the pages of an illustrated storybook. Was this what it was like to be a normal child? Was your whole life a multi-coloured blur of playrooms, classrooms, toys and books? Lizzie couldn't take it all in – she was deathly tired and the ordeal of the day was dragging at her. She shouldn't have done this. Readings always drained her. Her grip on the ribbon slackened, and the images began to fade.

No. Hold on just a little longer. She clutched the ribbon tightly, forcing herself to concentrate.

Just for a second, she saw her own face through Amelia's eyes. There were trees behind her. She heard the words 'hide and seek'.

It's earlier on today, she suddenly realized. She sat bolt upright.

Laughing happily, Amelia ran through the woods and Lizzie saw the huge oak tree lurch into her vision. It loomed larger and larger. There was a sudden blur – and Lizzie abruptly snapped out of the trance, gasping like a shipwrecked sailor clawing her way to shore.

Nobody spoke a word as Lizzie gulped down a whole mug of tea and wiped her mouth.

Then she sighed. 'Sorry. I tried my best.'

'You didn't see her ghost?' Hari asked.

For the first time that day, Lizzie felt a spark of hope. 'No. I saw through her eyes, into her past. That means she's still alive!'

'You're sure?'

'Positive, mate.'

Fergus stretched and reached for his hat. 'Well, you pack of ruffians have led me astray once again. I was on my way home, but it's back to the office for me – I've got tomorrow's headlines to write.' He yawned. 'I might get some sleep around dawn.'

For the Penny Gaff Gang, there was nothing left to do but take the weary walk back to the campsite. By the time they reached it, the stars were out. Silent caravans stood waiting for them, their windows dark.

'Nobody's waiting up for us,' Nora said.

'They probably got bored of waiting,' Malachy told her. 'It's gone midnight. Get some sleep while you can, everyone. There'll be hell to pay tomorrow.'

CHAPTER 11

Bang. Bang. Bang. The sound of knocking shattered Lizzie's sleep like a boot through her window.

She sat up groggily, her tousled hair spilling down her shoulders. The light coming in was dim, so Lizzie knew it must still be early morning.

'What?' she yelled.

'It's Malachy,' came the answer. 'You need to get up. Now.'

Lizzie groped her way out of bed and unbolted the top half of the door. Malachy stood on the step, his face grim.

'What's the emergency?' she said, still foggy-headed

from sleep. Memories of the day before circled like fish in muddy water. One of them flashed a fin: *Amelia*. 'Have they found her?'

'It's not that. It's Pop. He wants to see all of us that went on the fairy hunt. Big top, five minutes.'

Lizzie yawned. 'What time is it?'

'Time you were dressed.' Malachy went running off in the direction of the Sullivans' caravan.

Fitzy wasn't happy – Lizzie could tell from the look on Malachy's face and the way he sounded. More of the previous day's events came back to her, and she looked longingly at her warm bed, but she quickly pulled on the clothes she'd left in a heap on the floor – they felt rough as sackcloth in the cold of early morning. A quick glance in the mirror told her she looked dreadful. She could fix that easily in ten minutes, but she only had three. A few swipes with the hairbrush would have to do.

She ran across dew-sodden grass to the silent show tent. Fitzy was waiting for them, with his back turned like a schoolmaster. Only when every one of the Penny Gaff Gang had arrived did he turn around.

'I was a happy man yesterday, at first,' he said softly. 'For once, there was a magnificent article in the paper about us. Superb publicity.'

Lizzie sat trembling, waiting for the other shoe to drop.

'Our friend Fergus was true to his word,' Fitzy went on. 'He kept his promise. Some other people made me a promise too. They promised to be home on time.'

He held up a colourful poster showing the twins and Dru doing their Highland Fling stunt. GALA SUNDAY PERFORMANCE, it proclaimed.

Slowly Fitzy tore the poster in half lengthways. The sound of ripping paper made Lizzie's teeth clench. He crumpled the pieces into a ball and flung them over his shoulder. The pupils of his eyes were pinpoints of black fury. 'We had record ticket sales after that article, and we had to cancel the show!'

Lizzie hadn't even considered *that* possibility. The whole show called off? Her mouth fell open in surprise.

Fitzy noticed and rounded on her.

'Erin and Nora, missing! Colette and Dru, missing! Hari, missing!' With every 'missing' he smacked his fingers into his hand, making Lizzie flinch. 'I had to cancel the show or I'd have been laughed out of town! But they weren't just lined up around the street to see the show, oh no. Guess who the crowds had come to see.'

'I don't know,' Lizzie stammered.

'"*There is but one genuine psychic in Edinburgh, and that is Lizzie Brown of Fitzy's Circus,*"' Fitzy quoted mockingly. 'Sound familiar?'

Lizzie felt like she was falling through the ground into a bottomless pit. 'Oh Gawd.'

'Dozens of 'em!' shouted Fitzy. 'With pockets full of cash! Everyone wanted a reading from the Magnificent Lizzie Brown – only Lizzie Brown was off hunting for *fairies*!'

'Dad, let her get a word in!' Malachy protested.

'All right. But I'm not happy, Mal. With any of you.'

All the Penny Gaff Gang hung their heads. They all loved Fitzy and looked up to him, and Lizzie could tell they all felt as bad as she did that they'd disappointed him. It was down to her to say something.

'We're really sorry,' she began. Everyone quickly agreed. Fitzy stuck out his chin, folded his arms and said nothing. An apology was the least he could expect, she knew.

'We would have been back in time, honest we would,' she said. 'But Amelia went missing. Alexander MacDonald's daughter, remember? She ran off and disappeared, and we all searched for hours and couldn't find her, and then we had to talk to the police, and they kept us for ages, and by the time we got home we'd missed the show.'

'So you came straight back?'

'Well … no.' Lizzie fidgeted. 'We talked to Fergus first. He wants to help us find Amelia, Fitzy!'

'Let's get something clear, once and for all.' Fitzy rapped his cane against one of the central tent poles. 'Listen up, you lot. Yes, even you, Collette. I need to drum something into your thick skulls.'

They waited.

Fitzy threw his arms up towards the canvas roof over their heads, and bellowed, '*This* is your first responsibility. The circus. People here depend on you! You're not just taking money out of my pocket if you miss a show – you're betraying everyone. For some of you, that includes your own parents. Got that?'

'Yes,' they all mumbled.

'I know you're brave kids. You like to help people when you can, solving mysteries and what not. I'm proud of you for that, always will be. But there's no need to go looking for trouble. Savvy?'

'Circus comes first, Pop,' said Malachy. 'We won't

neglect our duties in future.'

'We promise!' Nora said. The Penny Gaff Gang all agreed loudly.

Lizzie followed them out of the tent, her heart aching. *I meant well,* she told herself. *I was only trying to help Amelia. That has to count for something, doesn't it?*

But it did nothing to ease the bitter, hollow feeling inside her. For the first time since he'd taken her on, she'd let Fitzy down. Now things could never be the same between them.

The tea tent was usually a place where Lizzie could hide away from the world. Within its colourful canvas walls, Ma Sullivan ruled like a kindly queen, and woe betide any circus member who brought a quarrel in under her roof. The show tent might be Fitzy's domain, but this was hers and everyone – Fitzy included – respected that.

This morning, however, Ma Sullivan found bad news waiting for her. Pa Sullivan was sitting at breakfast, reading the morning papers. The front page screamed: MACDONALD HEIRESS MISSING.

'Fergus got his scoop, then,' Malachy said.

'Poor wee thing,' Ma Sullivan sighed. As usual, she talked as she worked, helping the children to platefuls of porridge, fried bread, cooked tomatoes and eggs. 'I could have told that uncle of hers: don't go looking for trouble and trouble won't come looking for you.'

That's more or less what Fitzy told us, Lizzie thought. 'They were looking for fairies,' she said.

'Aye, and fairies are trouble!' Ma Sullivan muttered something under her breath, spat once on the floor and rummaged with something in her pocket. 'A fairy hunt, indeed! Where's the sense in that? They might as well have gone to play football with a wasp's nest. Leave the Good Folk well alone.'

'If fairies are so bad, why do you call them the Good Folk?' Lizzie asked, curious.

'To keep from offending them, my duck.' Ma Sullivan added a dollop of jam to Lizzie's porridge; it lay there like a ruby. *That's my reward for not mocking*, Lizzie thought to herself.

'They're not *bad*. Well, there's some that are bad through and through. You don't want to be running foul of evil spirits like Black Annis or a kelpie. But stay on their good side and you've no need to fear them.'

'Erin said fairies steal children,' Lizzie said. 'That doesn't sound very nice.'

'Oh, but the way the fairies see it, it's a kindness!' Ma Sullivan said. 'Some poor little human child gets to go to Fairyland, where they'll live for ever and be treated like a princess.'

Lizzie thought of Alexander MacDonald, desperate to find his niece. 'Not kind for their families, though.'

'The fairies leave behind a child of their own, in trade,' Ma Sullivan told her knowingly. 'I remember back home in Roscommon, there was a young couple who had a fairy mound in their back garden. Well, he was a fool of a man, and he went and dug into it in search of gold.'

'But he didn't find any,' Erin joined in excitedly. 'He just angered the fairies, so they took the couple's baby and left a changeling in its place!'

'A changeling?' Lizzie worked her tongue around the strange word.

'It may look like a human baby, but it's from the faerie folk,' said Ma Sullivan. 'Changelings are always ill-tempered. They howl and cry all the time. And if you walk out of the room, so the changeling thinks it's all alone, and if you listen carefully you can hear it laughing and talking to itself in a grown-up voice.'

Nora gave a horrified shudder. 'Imagine that! A little baby talking with a nasty old man's voice!'

Lizzie thought it sounded like a convenient explanation for children who wouldn't settle. No doubt many a mother blamed 'the fairies' for her screaming child.

'I see that look on your face, Lizzie Brown!' Ma Sullivan scowled. 'If you'd been in my kitchen yesterday, you could have seen fairies here in the flesh! This country is riddled with them.'

Nora and Erin gaped. 'You saw them, Ma?' they said together.

'I was that close.' She pinched her fingers together. 'I'd laid out some biscuits to cool, and when I came back in, a whole stack of 'em were gone!'

'Are you sure it wasn't Sean?' Lizzie asked with a smirk.

'It wasn't me!' Sean said, sounding genuinely shocked – but then he always did when you accused him of anything, whether he'd done it or not.

Ma Sullivan folded her arms triumphantly. 'And how could it be him, now, when the door was locked, and the only way in was through a wee tiny window?'

Lizzie finished the rest of her breakfast in a grumpy silence. Back in her caravan, she tidied herself up in preparation for a day of readings and her reflection looked back at her with sad eyes. Most days, Lizzie would whistle and sing as she brushed her hair, because she looked forward to her work. She pulled her weight at Fitzy's, and she was proud of it. The money was good, but it was helping people that she really enjoyed.

But as she changed into her mystic robes this grey morning, there was only one person she wanted to help. The search for Amelia would be well underway by now. First light, the constable had said. Lizzie's heart ached to be there with them, helping to search.

No point in asking Fitzy if she could join the search, though. She had a day of lost trade to make up for as it was. She made her way toward her little tent, and with a sinking heart saw the line of people already waiting.

'There's dozens of 'em,' she groaned, 'and we haven't even opened yet!'

By the time Lizzie's long, long shift was over, she was wishing she'd never let Fergus write his article. Calling her 'Edinburgh's only genuine psychic' had been a heck of a recommendation. Client after client had begged for her advice, until she had had to add a new rule: only fifteen minutes per client! Even then, many of them overstayed their time and Malachy had to fetch Bungo to persuade them to leave.

In the end, the only thing that stopped the constant trade was the start of the show in the main tent. Lizzie looked outside, saw nobody waiting and heard Fitzy's voice welcoming the huge crowds to the evening's performance.

Phew. She collapsed back into her seat, feeling like a wrung-out dishrag. It was dark again, so the search for Amelia would be over by now for today. Surely if the searchers had found anything, Fergus would have come and told her?

There had to be something she could do to help. She felt in her pocket and pulled out Amelia's hair ribbon. Yesterday, she'd seen Amelia's memories through her own eyes. Maybe today she might catch a flash of where she was now? Even if it was only a second's glimpse, it had to be worth a try…

She concentrated and a vision instantly blossomed into life in her mind.

She saw the huge oak tree and Amelia dancing. No, she wasn't just dancing – she was chasing someone. High, bright laughter trilled through the air. A figure was vanishing around the tree. It wore a shimmering dress of diaphanous material and on its back was a blur of colour like butterfly wings.

'Come here, fairy!' called Amelia.

The silvery laugh came again and then there was the sound of singing: 'O fairies true, join us do…'

The song no longer sounded silly. It was mischievous, even sinister – it was everything Ma Sullivan had said fairies were. Lizzie had to get a clear look at the fairy. She strained to see—

Sudden as a snapping stick, the vision ended. The curtain to Lizzie's tent opened.

'What? Who's there?' Caught between two worlds, Lizzie floundered for a moment. Then she saw it was only Collette, peering in with concern. She rubbed her eyes. 'Sorry. I was having one of my turns.'

'May I come in?'

'Course you can. Aren't you meant to be in the show tonight?'

Collette winced as she sat down. 'My back is 'urting too much. But my heart 'urts worse.'

'It's Amelia, isn't it?'

Collette nodded, her eyes glistening in the candlelight. 'I want her to be all right. I am so worried about her.'

Lizzie must have let the surprise show on her face, because Collette quickly added, 'I love *les enfants*! All of them. You did not know?'

'To be honest, you're so glamorous I never thought you were the type.'

Collette shrugged – *just like Dru*, Lizzie thought – and gave a rueful little smile. 'I cannot wait to have children of my own.' She sighed deeply. 'But it is hard to find a husband when you are always on the move, *hein*.'

Lizzie hesitated, wondering if she could trust Collette, and came to a decision. It would be easier if she just said it all at once. 'I saw Amelia just now, in my vision. She was dancing around a tree. With a fairy.'

'A fairy,' Collette repeated. Her eyes widened.

'I know!' Lizzie burst out. 'Every time someone says fairies have taken Amelia, I've been calling 'em stupid, but what if that's what really happened?' She flailed her hands as she grappled with the idea. 'I can't call it stupid if I've seen it myself, can I? Maybe fairies really *do* exist!'

'Seeing is believing,' Collette murmured.

'I used to think ghosts were hogwash – then I started talking to them. Erin's right. You can't stay a sceptic after that.'

The memory of the last ghost she'd spoken to surfaced in Lizzie's mind: Amelia's mother. *Beware the fairy*, she'd said.

Lizzie sprang up out of her chair. 'Oh gawd. Her uncle! That fairy ... I have to tell Alexander MacDonald what I just saw.'

'So what are we waiting for?' Collette threw her shawl over her shoulders.

'We?'

'*Naturellement.* I will come too.'

CHAPTER 12

Lizzie was grateful for Collette's company as they made their way out of the park and into the sprawling, unfamiliar city.

The lamplighters had already made their rounds and a welcome glow of yellow gaslight shone down from the cast-iron pillars. At night Edinburgh was a different place, a labyrinth of stone buildings and rowdy noises.

There were crowds everywhere. If Lizzie had been on her own, she would have shrunk into herself, hurrying along with her eyes downcast. Every yell, every laugh, would have made her nervous. But somehow Collette seemed to hold the night at bay.

Lizzie smiled to see the determined look on her friend's face. Who would have thought that the two of them would become friends? When Lizzie had first joined the circus, Collette had been bitter and mean-spirited – or so it had seemed. Now Lizzie understood she was just protective of her brother, Dru.

Lizzie and Collette passed pubs that were packed wall to wall, brawny men singing and arm-wrestling, and crumbling houses with women leaning out of the top windows.

So many people, Lizzie thought, *and not enough room for them.* There couldn't be enough work to go around, either.

'What are you going to do about your back?' she asked Collette. 'You can't keep performing if it's giving you grief.'

Collette sighed. 'I have to earn my keep somehow, Lizzie. The family business is what I know best.'

'But there must be something else you can do!'

'*Non.* I can work, or I can find a husband. There is nothing else.'

They swerved to cross the street away from a young man who was swinging on a lamppost. He winked at Collette, who walked straight ahead and pretended she hadn't seen him.

'Animals,' she muttered, once the youth was out of earshot.

Lizzie struggled to think what else Collette could do with her life. Some young women worked as nursemaids, of course, like Maisie had done. But Maisie had been thrown out into the street, without even a reference to help her find new work. Was she out here somewhere, in a poorhouse or worse? She wouldn't be working in service ever again, not after MacDonald's grim treatment. Perhaps some young man would make her his wife…

Lizzie mulled that over as she walked. So much in a woman's life depended on men, for there were precious few paths open to an unmarried woman. Factory work was just about the only option, without a reference, and she knew how very lucky she was to have found work at Fitzy's Circus. Lizzie wasn't sure whether she wanted to get married one day, but one thing was for sure – thanks to her abilities, she'd never have to be someone's wife unless that was what *she* wanted.

Collette and Lizzie passed into the narrow, seedy streets of the Grassmarket, a low-lying part of the city where squalid houses pressed together back to back.

The castle loomed above, high on its craggy column of rock, a forbidding outline against the night sky.

Only the main street was well lit. Narrow, dark alleys led off to the left and right, their shadowy openings somehow both threatening and tempting. There were women in the alleyways, she saw now. They leaned against the walls, weary or drunk or probably both. One had a face pitted with pox scars, another had a black eye, and another a crooked jaw that must have been broken long ago.

There were alleys like this back in Rat's Castle, where she'd grown up, and she knew how easily she could have ended up like that one of those women in a few years, shivering and bone-thin, slumped against the cobblestones with only the false warmth of alcohol to keep the cold away.

Silently Lizzie thanked whatever kindly power had changed the course of her life. Thanks to Fitzy's Circus, she had an honest living. More than that, she had her freedom.

Walking briskly on, she followed Collette up the hill and out of the slums – eager to leave the all-too-familiar squalor behind.

* * *

In the porch of Alexander MacDonald's elegant house, Lizzie pulled the bell rope. She heard a bell ring somewhere deep inside, many rooms away.

A minute later, a stony-faced housekeeper opened the door. 'Mister MacDonald is not receiving visitors.'

'But it's me,' Lizzie protested. 'Lizzie Brown, the psychic. I want to help.'

'Help?' roared a voice from the end of the hall. 'That girl has "helped" quite enough already!' Alexander MacDonald came striding up the hall towards her, clutching a candlestick. His hair was in disarray and his eyes sunken and bloodshot. *He looks half-mad*, Lizzie thought with alarm.

'I had a vision…'

'Spare me. I should never have entrusted my niece to the care of a circus girl. *Get out.*'

The door slammed in Lizzie's face.

Lizzie looked from the door to Collette and back again. 'What am I supposed to do now?'

'Don't give up,' Collette said.

'Come off it. The jig's up. He doesn't want to talk to me and I can't make him. Let's go home.' She pulled the ribbon out of her pocket. 'At least I've still got this.'

Collette ushered her away from the door and spoke in a whisper. 'The ribbon – it works as a link, *oui*? For your visions?'

'Yes.'

'So what if we could get inside the house? To Amelia's nursery? Surely that would be a link as strong as iron!'

Lizzie boggled at the idea. 'It'd be worth a try, if there was any chance of getting in, which there ain't.'

Collette tugged her across the courtyard and looked up at the windows. 'Show me which one it is.'

'It's the middle one,' Lizzie said, pointing. 'She waved to me from the window.'

'*Bon. Regarde moi.*'

In the shadows of the courtyard, Collette seemed to transform. The young woman who was as graceful as a swan on the flying trapeze suddenly seemed more like a cat, with quick eyes and a wicked grin. She darted straight to the stone-clad space between two tall windows, where ivy draggled down, and began to climb.

Lizzie watched dumbfounded as Collette pulled herself up, one stone block at a time. There were little metal balconies outside all the upper windows, and soon Collette was able to grasp one from below and swing nimbly up and over. She crouched and beckoned.

With a gulp, Lizzie took hold of a crevice in the stone and began to climb. She could hear voices from inside the house, just beyond the window. If she fell, they'd hear the crash. And it would hurt.

'Put your right foot *there*,' hissed Collette. '*Bien*. Move your left hand *there*. No. More to the left. That's it. Now pull!'

It was hard work and Lizzie was soon sweating despite the chill. Last time she'd had to climb up a house, it had been Dru coaching her and he'd ended up in Newgate prison. Fortunately Lizzie's visions had helped her to catch the real culprit, a masked burglar known as the Phantom. It had made Lizzie's name, and she said a silent prayer that her success continued.

Inch by inch, she scaled up the side of the building until the balcony was within reach. Without waiting for Collette's prompt, she reached for it – and immediately lost her balance. Unable to stop herself, she let out a yell. She was going to fall!

Collette grabbed her by the wrist. Grimacing with pain, she pulled Lizzie up and onto the balcony beside her. They both crouched down, breathing hard, terrified that the front door would open.

'It seems they did not hear us,' Collette eventually whispered. 'Help me open the window. After three…'

Just then, a metallic clang made them jump. The main gates were swinging open. A whip cracked, and a horse-drawn carriage came rattling into the courtyard from the street. Two lanterns at the front lit up the front of the house in a wide arc.

Collette ducked down behind the ornate metalwork of the balcony and pulled Lizzie down next to her. They huddled in the shadows.

A door opened in the side of the carriage and a man got out, his face obscured by a hat pulled down low. The light from the lanterns was dazzling. If the figure looked up, would he see them? Lizzie had no way to know.

The visitor took a step towards the house, then paused. Lizzie froze, not daring to breathe. The door opened, flooding the porch with light, and Lizzie heard voices talking, but couldn't make out the words. The figure moved out of view.

'Now!' Collette urged. 'While they're busy!'

They tugged the bedroom window up. It made a grinding squeak, just as the front door shut with a bang, muffling the sound completely. Lizzie grinned at their good luck. One after the other, they crept in through the window, treading carefully on the carpeted floor for fear of creaking floorboards.

Amelia's nursery was like the front window of a toyshop. It was stiflingly warm, with a smell of rose petals and lavender. More of Charles Doyle's fairy pictures hung from the walls, each one showing beautiful fairy women opening their arms in welcome. The shelves were overflowing with picture books, while porcelain dolls sat propped up on the bed and against the wall, watching Lizzie with dead, glassy eyes.

Collette opened the wardrobe and whistled softly. Masses of brightly coloured silk and satin dresses hung there. Lizzie had no idea when Amelia found time to wear them all, even if she wore a new one to every tea party she had.

'No wonder she's mad for fairies,' Lizzie whispered. She tried to imagine what it must be like, growing up in such luxury. There didn't seem to be room for a real, human little girl among all this frippery and splendour. The heat and the smell of flowers were making her head spin, so she lay down on Amelia's bed. It was like sinking into a mountain of feathers.

'Do you see anything?' Collette asked eagerly.

'No.'

As Collette paced up and down, Lizzie closed her eyes and tried to imagine Amelia here in the room. *Alive.*

Immediately the doors of her mind were flung open. Lizzie whimpered a little; it was a vision, and it was a powerful one – and she was seeing it through Amelia's eyes.

She was in a dark room. 'I want to go home,' Amelia's voice whimpered. Fresh, hot tears ran down her face.

'Hush, now,' said a strange, hollow voice. 'Don't be scared, my little elf.'

Lizzie tried to send her thoughts to Amelia. *Turn around,* she thought. *Show me where that voice is coming from!* But the little girl just kept crying.

The voice began to sing.

'Where the bee sucks, there suck I.

In a cowslip's bell I lie.

On a bat's back I do fly…'

'Lizzie!' Collette hissed.

The vision faded away and Lizzie sat up. There were voices coming from downstairs; she heard MacDonald and another man – and the creak, creak, creak of footsteps coming up the stairs!

Lizzie and Collette exchanged alarmed glances. Collette glanced at the window, but Lizzie shook her head. She quickly climbed into the wardrobe and wriggled down among the heaps of stifling silk. Collette climbed in after her and pulled the door shut, just as the bedroom door opened.

Lizzie heard the men enter Amelia's room. To her horror, she saw Collette had closed the armoire door on a dress sleeve and it hadn't shut properly. A half-inch crack now showed her a view of the room.

As the visitor crossed the room, she saw his face clearly. It was the famous medium – her enemy, Douglas Grant.

He breathed in deeply through his nose. 'I can sense Amelia's aura – very close, very strong. Her innocent life force has impressed itself upon the room.' He sank down onto the bed and clutched his head. His face contorted in pain.

Pull the other one, Lizzie thought. *You might fool MacDonald, but you don't fool me.*

'What is it?' MacDonald said, hovering nearby. 'Do you see her?'

Grant dabbed at his sweating forehead. 'I must ask

you for a brandy,' he gasped. 'What I have seen … I pray it is not true, and yet in my heart I know that it is.'

'Is it bad news?' MacDonald asked bravely.

'Deeply worrying, my friend. Let me have a restorative drink, and I shall tell you what I have seen.'

The two men left the room.

'We've got to sneak downstairs,' Lizzie whispered.

'*Non!*' Collette said sharply.

'Yes! I need to know what that faker Grant is telling him!'

'And if we are caught? What then? We would be arrested, charged with breaking and entering! You think Fitzy needs that, *hein*?'

Lizzie groaned 'If I could just listen at the door…'

'And hear what? Grant is a fake. Whatever he tells MacDonald will be a pack of lies. He'll probably say that Amelia is a changeling, and that the fairies took her back or some such nonsense.'

'I suppose you're right,' Lizzie sighed. 'Come on.'

They eased the window open, more gently this time. Silently they clambered out onto the balcony. As Grant's carriage was waiting beneath the window and the driver was nowhere in sight, they jumped down onto its roof instead of risking the wall climb again.

Lizzie glanced over her shoulder at the house, yearning to hear what was being said within its walls. Grant was up to something. But what was it?

CHAPTER 13

The next morning, Lizzie was up early. Although she wouldn't have any customers until the afternoon, she was sure she could find a way to be helpful. She wanted to show Fitzy how important the circus was to her. As she hurried to the tea tent, Lizzie spotted a familiar face.

'Morning, Fergus!'

The journalist didn't return Lizzie's greeting. He just kept walking towards her, a stack of newspapers under his arm and a grim look on his face.

Lizzie sagged. 'If it's bad news, can it wait until I've had breakfast?'

'I'll join you, if I may. Haven't slept all night. Could use a strong cup of tea.'

They headed for the tea tent, side by side, unlikely allies. Lizzie decided she had to know how bad it was.

'Come on, then. Let's have it. Spit it out.'

In answer, Fergus showed her the front page of the *Edinburgh Gazette.*

FAMOUS PSYCHIC JOINS SEARCH FOR MISSING HEIRESS, howled the headline.

At first, Lizzie wondered how the paper knew about her wanting to help. Then she saw the huge picture of Douglas Grant, and the penny dropped.

'Show me!' She all but snatched the paper out of Fergus's hands and read the section: '*Acclaimed medium Douglas Grant has put his long-proven psychic abilities at Alexander MacDonald's service,*' she read. 'Long-proven, my backside!'

'Read the rest,' Fergus said quietly.

Lizzie skimmed through it. 'Blah blah, famous medium, blah blah psychic vibrations – wait. *Grant has already had an important breakthrough, in the form of a compelling vision of the girl's abductor?*' That must be the 'vision' she'd seen Grant having last night. 'Who's he seen?'

'Have a guess.'

Lizzie's grip tightened on the pages. *'According to Mr Grant, the missing heiress was abducted by a young, thin female of a working-class demeanour. Her hair is described as ...* long and light brown?'

'Keep reading,' said Fergus. 'There's more.'

'Only one person on the doomed fairy hunt matches Mr Grant's description,' Lizzie read, *'and that is the supposedly "Magnificent" Lizzie Brown, a member of a troupe of circus performers. We are informed that Miss Brown was the last known person to have seen little Amelia.'*

Back in Rat's Castle, people rarely taunted Lizzie twice. She might be skinny, but she could fight dirty when she had to. That was how it was in the slum – it was you or the other fella. She stood now, baring her teeth, sucking air in through her nose. If Grant had been in front of her then, she would have chopped his head clean off and booted it like a football over the top of Arthur's Seat. Or so she told herself.

'He can't bloomin' well say that about me!' she yelled.

Fergus shrugged. 'The papers are old hands at this game, lass. They're careful. Read it again. They haven't actually *said* that you're the abductor.

They've just implied it.'

Lizzie stormed ahead of him. She strode straight into the tea tent, where a group of her friends were eating an early breakfast, and slammed the paper down on the table. Teacups jumped in their saucers.

'DOUGLAS FLAMIN' GRANT!' she screeched at the alarmed faces. 'He's only gone and had a fake vision and called *me* the abductor, ain't he? I'm going to smash his ruddy face in, I swear to God!'

'Lizzie,' Malachy said in a low, calm voice, 'sit down, take a deep breath, and have a cup of tea.' Lizzie knew the look in his eye – it was the same one his father had while he was taming the circus lion.

'I'll get it!' Collette sprang up eagerly. 'Tea, Fergus?'

'I'd be much obliged, Mademoiselle Boisset,' the journalist said with a grin. 'It will help me stay awake.' *Was it just the thought of a cup of tea that had suddenly made him perk up*, Lizzie wondered. *Or was it the sight of the pretty French trapeze artist?*

As Lizzie strode back and forth, still too angry to sit down, Malachy picked over the article. 'Hmm,' he said. 'Aha. Yes.' And then, 'It's possible.'

After five minutes of this, during which Collette flitted back and forth bringing Fergus tea and cake and a napkin and finally a flapjack, Lizzie had had enough. 'You've got a new notion, ain't you, Mal? Let's hear it.'

'What if,' Malachy said, 'it was Grant who took Amelia, or arranged for her to be taken?'

Lizzie could believe it of him, the wretched weaselly liar.

'But why?' Fergus asked.

'So he can lead the police straight to wherever he's got her hidden, then claim his powers told him where to find her. Hey presto – Grant looks like a hero, *and* he proves he's Edinburgh's top psychic into the bargain.'

'That makes sense!' Lizzie said, hating Grant more than ever. 'If he's put Amelia through all this just to get at me … ooh, I'll kill him, mate. I mean it.'

Fergus took out his notebook. 'If you like, I'll put your side of the story in the *Gazette* tomorrow.' He drew an imaginary headline in the air. '*War of the Psychics: My personal agony, by falsely accused fortune-teller.* Something like that.'

'Thanks, but no. I don't want any more newspaper stories about me. To tell you the truth, I've had a ruddy gutful of newspapers.'

* * *

This day's going from bad to worse, Lizzie thought as she frantically searched her fortune-telling tent. Her favourite crystal ball was missing. It was a small one, slightly cracked, and she liked it better than the perfect ones. She didn't actually need a crystal ball to see into the future, but it looked impressive and she liked the feel of it in her hand.

'I could swear I left it right here!' she muttered.

A soft splat on the outside of her tent made her pause. Then another, and another. Rain? No, the splats were too heavy and far apart.

She sniffed. A stench like an open sewer was filling her tent. She stuck her head outside, then whipped it back in quickly as a volley of rotten eggs came flying towards her along with howls and jeers.

'Bring her back!'

'Kidnapper!'

'Fraud!'

All Lizzie could do was hide inside her tent and wait for someone to shoo them away. Grant had poisoned the crowd against her – that much was obvious. There would be no readings today.

Eventually the egging stopped. Lizzie waited for

five long minutes before working up the nerve to go outside. Her poor little tent was plastered with stinking muck. Nothing would get the smell out – it would have to be burned.

Suddenly the thought hit her: *It won't just be me who loses trade! Who's going to take their children to a circus where a suspected kidnapper is on the loose?*

She found Fitzy in his caravan. The gloomy look on his face told the whole story. As did a copy of the *Edinburgh Gazette*, open to Grant's article, which lay to one side.

'Bloomin' papers,' he said, with a sigh. 'Should have known it was too good to last.'

'How bad is it?' Lizzie managed to ask.

'We've sold a few tickets for tonight. I suppose we *might* sell a few more.'

That 'might' burned in Lizzie's stomach like indigestion. 'I haven't got any customers for today,' she said, thinking of Amelia. 'Is it all right if I—'

Fitzy flashed her a dangerous look.

'...go and help Hari with the animals?' Lizzie finished.

'Of course,' Fitzy said. 'Help out wherever you like. Always plenty to do at Fitzy's Circus. You know that.'

'I do. Thanks, boss.'

For the rest of the afternoon, Lizzie helped out everywhere she could. She did the washing up for Ma Sullivan, fetched water for the elephants, refastened guy ropes that had come untied, and even hauled sacks full of rubbish off the campsite to the dumping area. All around, the stench of rotten eggs still clung, as if Grant had laid a curse on the circus.

The show that night was miserable. Only a handful of people turned up – and there were even less people than they had expected, because some who had bought tickets in advance changed their minds and stayed away. It hurt Lizzie's heart to think people would rather lose the price of a ticket than be seen at Fitzy's tonight.

'I've had worse turnouts,' JoJo the clown assured her behind the scenes. 'This one time in Cardiff, the only folk who turned up were three veterans from the Crimean War. Two of 'em was blind, and one was deaf! But we still gave 'em a show.'

'The show must go on,' agreed Mario the strong man. 'Chin up, Liz. It ain't your fault. It's that scrawny blighter in the papers. If I ever get my hands on that Douglas Grant...' He tucked a walnut between his forearm and bicep, grunted and flexed. There was a loud crunch, Mario grinned and Lizzie cheered.

Later, as the show struggled through its second act, Lizzie sat watching from the wings, her head in her hands. Malachy came and joined her.

'It's not your fault,' he said.

'Everybody says that,' she snapped, 'and it's getting a bit hard to believe 'em.'

'But you've done nothing wrong! Nobody blames you…'

'I started it,' Lizzie said. 'I called Grant a fraud. Should have left well alone.'

'But he *is* a fraud.'

Lizzie glanced at Malachy's club foot. 'You walk with a crutch. But if anyone called you a cripple, you'd deck them for it.'

Malachy chuckled and shook his head. 'Have it your way.'

Lizzie stuck it out until the circus had finished, and the smattering of half-hearted applause had died down. The audience left and Fitzy took off his hat and threw it wearily aside. 'Thank God that's over,' he said. 'Well done, all. Go and get some rest.'

Not for the first time, Lizzie wondered if this was the price of her fortune-telling powers. She was one in a million, a genuine psychic – but every time she used her powers for good, other people suffered. She'd tried to expose Grant as a fraud and help the man he was swindling – Alexander MacDonald – but once again the circus was out of pocket. If this kept up, they'd have to move to another city sooner than planned.

She retreated to her caravan and threw herself into bed. Tired as she was, sleep should have come straight away. But it didn't.

Minutes passed. She struggled to fall asleep, tossing and turning. Her pillow felt too big, so she threw it onto the floor.

The minutes stretched into hours. The moon was bright outside the window. Lizzie grabbed her pillow back again and buried her face in it.

She tried to count imaginary sheep. She tried lying on her back, on her side, on her front. The more she thought about falling asleep, the more she knew she wouldn't. Thinking about it just made it worse.

The night dragged past hour by miserable hour. Lizzie stared at the ceiling. Gradually the night sky outside the window became a dim rectangle of grey. 'Sun's coming up,' she mumbled. 'Might as well get dressed. No point staying in bed if

I'm not going to sleep.'

In the dim half-light, she groped for something to tie her hair back, and her fingers closed on Amelia's ribbon.

Instantly a vision struck her, crystal-clear. It was the future – and she was seeing it through Amelia's eyes!

Someone behind her was shoving her through a door, into the roaring, clattering hell of a factory. She heard a loud whistle blow and felt Amelia's terror, heard her heart pounding hard. 'No,' Amelia's voice whimpered. 'Don't make me go inside!'

Lizzie sat bolt upright in bed, gasping. Her heart was still hammering as if she'd woken up from a nightmare. And yet, through the fear, she felt a wild triumph.

'I know that place!' she said. 'It's the MacDonald woollen mill!' She'd seen it on the train journey to the fairy hunt – Amelia had been so proud of it.

She threw herself out of bed. Amelia was going to be taken to the mill! She knew it with a deep, iron certainty.

And that meant that only one person could be responsible.

She pulled her clothes on, her thoughts coming fast and furious. 'MacDonald,' she said. 'You're behind this. I could have sworn you'd have died to protect Amelia, but you're as much of a fraud as your chum Grant, aren't you?' She gave herself a vicious smack on the forehead. 'Idiot! When are you going to learn? Just because someone seems nice, it doesn't mean they are!'

MacDonald's motive was clear. He wanted the whole mill for himself. For that to happen, Amelia had to die. Lizzie felt sick to her stomach as she realized he must be taking her to the mill to kill her. Probably he'd fake an accident, or hide her body in a bundle of cloth … Lizzie wasn't sure what he'd done with his niece since the picnic – but when a man was that rich he could afford to pay someone to do his dirty work. She could only imagine where Amelia had been these past few days.

'I've got to stop him!' she moaned. She had to get to the MacDonald mill, and fast.

She quickly scribbled a note – *HAD VISION. GONE TO MILL TO SAVE AMELIA. SORRY* – and ran and slipped it under Fitzy's caravan door. Then she was running through the Edinburgh streets as the sun rose, heading for Waverley station.

CHAPTER 14

Lizzie huddled up on the train seat with her head pressed against the cold glass of the window. Last time she'd made this journey, all her friends had been here. Soon they would be waking up, and word would go round about what she had done. Lizzie flinched as she thought how hurt they'd all be, especially Malachy.

They were a gang; they worked together. She knew she should have told them about her plan to save Amelia. But if she had, they'd be here now, heading into all sorts of danger. No. Fitzy's Circus had suffered enough because of her. She'd make this journey on her own.

The train made its fitful journey out of Edinburgh. Stop followed stop, and more passengers squeezed on board at every station. The carriage windows steamed up and Lizzie had to rub a hole in the mist so she could watch for the mill.

She needn't have worried about missing it. As the grim shape of the mill came into view, the train slowed down, then came to a screeching halt and a few passengers piled out.

Breathing fresh air again at last, Lizzie went and stood on the footbridge over the tracks and looked out across the town. All around, the cramped cottages and packed boarding houses were emptying people out onto the street. Everyone, it seemed, was heading to work at the same place.

No need to ask anyone the way. Lizzie just climbed back down and followed the flow of people down a cobbled, mud-strewn road. At the end of the road, the mill loomed like a forbidding castle.

A shrill whistle pierced the air – the sound she'd heard in her vision. Lizzie jumped. Everyone else quickened their pace, moving like weary cattle towards the mill gates. That must be the signal for the work day to begin, Lizzie realized.

What to do now? Amelia was inside there, somewhere. She might be inside that tall tower, or under the sloping, colossal vault of the roof. Lizzie rubbed her bleary eyes and tried to think clearly. She had to get inside.

The easiest thing to do was just let herself be borne on the human river, tramping with the rest of the people up the path, through the gates and into the factory. Surely nobody would be surprised at a new mill girl arriving for her first day at work? Lizzie decided she could bluff her way through.

The main doors were already open. The din of working machinery was worse than the sound of the steam trains. Beyond, a tile-floored hallway waited, where people were hanging up coats. Lizzie didn't have a coat, so she shuffled to one side and waited to see what would happen next.

A friendly-looking girl tapped her on the shoulder. She was about Lizzie's age, with crow-black hair and sharp bony features, as if she'd missed a few too many meals for her own good.

The girl smiled and shouted above the noise 'I'm Fiona! First day?'

Lizzie nodded. 'I'm Liz.'

Fiona cupped her hand to her ear. 'Eh?'

'Liz!' yelled Lizzie.

'I'm deaf as a post,' Fiona explained. 'From the machines. Anyhow, you needn't fret. I've been here ages. I'll show you where to go.'

She led Lizzie by the hand into the factory itself.

Nothing could have prepared Lizzie for this. It was like a church, but a church built to the Devil instead of to God. Heat blasted you as soon as you walked in, making your eyes feel like dried-out baps. The noise shook you to the very bones, rattling your teeth against your skull, threatening to shake them loose, and the whole place stank of oil, scorched metal and hot wool.

All down the length of the place, to the left and right, gigantic machines stood. Some were like huge engines, with wheels spinning and pistons pumping. Some were frames that clattered and clacked, champing like monstrous jaws, steadily vomiting out cloth. And all were tethered in place by bolts that could have restrained a giant.

The air was filled with dust and fibres. Lizzie took a breath and began to cough. Many of the workers had tied scarves round their mouths, she saw.

'Which machine are you workin'?' Fiona shouted.

Lizzie panicked. She had no idea what to say. 'I don't know yet!' she blurted.

'Don't worry, pet. We'd best take you to see Dimmock. He's the boss.'

Dimmock turned out to be a small, balding man with a jutting lower jaw, which gave him a surly look, and little piggy eyes behind round glasses. He looked Lizzie up and down and pinched the flesh of her arm as if she were a heifer he was buying at the market.

'Show us your fingers,' he demanded.

Lizzie did.

'Look nimble enough. Set her up on the spinning mule,' he told Fiona. 'She'll do for a piecer.'

'Can I have a word with Mister MacDonald first?' Lizzie said quickly.

'You? Speak to him?' Dimmock laughed in her face. 'Plannin' to ask for a raise, were ye? Get to work!'

'But I—'

'Waste one more second of my time, girl, and I'll whip you to the bone.'

Fiona dragged her away. 'He means it,' she warned. 'He's whipped girls and boys till the flesh came away. Come on, let me show you what you've got to do.'

Lizzie was led to a spinning mule, a machine that

spun fibres into yarn. One half of it rolled continually away from the other half on metal wheels and then back again, stretching dozens and dozens of fine threads between the two sides. Little children scurried back and forth under the machine, grabbing up fistfuls of fibres that had fallen out, then scrabbling back just in time. The wheels rolling back and forth seemed about to crush them at any second.

Lizzie stared dumbstruck at the thing.

'Watch it like a hawk,' Fiona said, 'and mend any broken threads you see. You've got to be quick. If you're slower than a count of ten, the spindle can jam and you'll hold the whole work up.'

'Mend them how? Tie them in a knot?'

'Heavens, no! Rub the fibres together. Like this.'

Quick as a pickpocket, Fiona snatched up two broken halves of a thread. A quick rub between finger and thumb, and the thread was whole again. It had taken all of three seconds.

'Fast in, fast out, see? But mind your hair and your fingers! Those spindles will wind whatever gets caught in 'em and they won't stop for all your screaming.'

Lizzie stared. 'You're kidding me.'

Fiona shook her head. 'Just last week a girl got

a patch of her scalp torn away. Big as your palm, it was. She'll no' forget to tie her hair back again, what's left of it.'

'Does that happen a lot?'

'Och, no. Most people only lose fingers.'

Lizzie shuddered and set to work.

Clackety-clack, clackety-clack, sang the machines. Minute after minute, hour after hour, nothing happened to relieve the boredom. Lizzie stood braced to snatch up any broken threads and mend them. The first time she'd managed it, it had been a thrill. After the twentieth time, she was aching and bored, but she didn't dare take her eyes off the machine.

Her nose and throat burned from the dust and fibres. How could the workers stand it? Obviously they had no choice. The pittance they were paid was better than the workhouse.

The morning seemed to stretch on for ever. Lizzie began to glance away from the spinning mule, hoping to catch sight of Amelia – the threads would just have to take care of themselves.

'You! Yes, you! Do you call that working?' Dimmock came striding over and Lizzie hastily went back to work, hoping he wasn't talking about her.

He wasn't. A small boy three rows down screamed as Dimmock hoisted him up by the scruff of the neck. The overseer carried him across the factory floor and plunged him into a cistern of ice-cold water. The boy struggled as Dimmock held him under. Just when Lizzie thought the boy would drown, Dimmock let him up, then flung him onto the floor. The boy lay there, gasping, retching up water.

'That'll wake you up,' Dimmock sneered. 'If I catch you slacking again, it'll be the whip!'

With the boy's howls ringing in her ears, Lizzie picked up her pace. She was starving, she realized. She'd run to the train station without eating anything, and after her sleepless night, she felt hungry and dead on her feet. Maybe there would be a break for lunch. The thought excited her. She could sneak away into the building and look for Amelia!

But lunch, when it finally came, was oat cakes and milk on a trolley. Nobody was allowed to leave.

'You eat standing up at your work,' Fiona told her. 'Boss's orders.'

Lizzie was so hungry she munched the dry oat cakes without a word of complaint. Fiona chatted away in the meantime, asking how she was getting along. 'You'll get used to it,' she assured her. 'You're not soft. I can tell.'

'What happens to the soft ones?'

Fiona shrugged. 'They toughen up. Or they get kicked out and take to begging.'

'Have you been working here long?'

'Since I was eight. I'm thirteen now.'

Trying to sound casual, Lizzie asked, 'Don't suppose you've seen a little girl? About so high, long blond hair.'

'I couldn't say,' Fiona said, shrugging again. 'There's so many wee 'uns at the mill they all blend into one.'

'Back to work!' Dimmock was hollering. 'What you've not bit off, you can't keep! Back to work!'

Even after the oat cakes, Lizzie's stomach was still grumbling. She tried not to think about what Ma Sullivan would be serving in the tea tent right about now...

* * *

The afternoon passed much as the morning did. A girl on one of the weaving looms had begun to sing a song that went 'poverty, poverty knock', fitting the words to the rhythm of her machine. But Dimmock had whipped her in front of everyone, lashing at her arms and back until she was forced to her knees, and there was no more singing after that.

Lizzie felt numb as a wooden toy. The work never changed. Hour followed monotonous hour. She picked up broken threads, rubbed them together, let them go, then did it all over again.

Around three o'clock the light through the tall windows began to fade. 'Spark the lamps!' came Dimmock's shout, and oil lamps were lit all around the factory.

It was growing late, and Lizzie still hadn't had a chance to look for Amelia. What if the girl was hidden in some other part of the mill? MacDonald could be cutting her throat while Lizzie wasted her time slaving over a spinning mule. She worried so much that she missed a broken thread, and the spindle had to be stopped.

Dimmock bore down on her. 'Idling, were ye?'

'I'm sorry, sir!' she stammered.

'I'm wanting another scavenger,' he barked. 'Down on the floor with you. Get under the machinery with them other kids and gather up all the scraps of wool. Understand?'

'Yes, sir.'

Lizzie trembled with a mix of excitement – and fear. Scavenging sounded like a dangerous job, but it meant she could finally look around. This was her chance to find Amelia!

CHAPTER 15

Lizzie crawled under the taut web of threads. Along with the other children, she pressed herself to the floor as the machinery rolled over her head. It rumbled back the other way and she quickly pulled herself forwards, snatching up wisps of stray wool as she went.

Down here, she was out of Dimmock's line of sight. With luck, she could slip out without him suspecting anything. As for what came next ... well, she'd just have to make it up as she went along.

She crawled back and forth for five minutes, gathering wool, just to be on the safe side. Her knees and elbows felt scraped raw, and for one terrifying second she felt a tug on the back of her head as the machinery passed over. She winced as a few hairs were torn out.

It sickened her to think there was nothing to protect her, nor any of the other children, except for quick reflexes. The rolling mass of machinery would crush a child's head as easily as a fairground coconut.

Now, she thought. Quick as a ferret, she scurried out from under the spinning mule and behind the sheltering mass of a weaving machine. A few pairs of eyes glanced her way, but to her immense relief nobody shouted an alarm.

There was a gantry up above, running around the outside of the room. If she could get up there somehow, she could look for Amelia among the crowds of workers. Her honey-coloured hair should be easy to see.

The ladder up to the gantry was on the other side of the factory. To get there, she'd have to run across an open area. Dimmock, who sat on a platform at the end watching like a Cyclops, would be sure to see her. She needed another plan.

She peeped out from behind the machine. No sign of Amelia anywhere.

But then she noticed the door of dark wood up by

Dimmock's platform and the shiny brass plaque affixed to it. A. MACDONALD, it read.

Of course. Why in God's name had she been looking for Amelia on the factory floor? There, the workers would recognize the missing girl, whose photograph had been in all the newspapers. Her uncle must be hiding her in his office!

Determination made her bold. The whale-oil lamps lit up most of the factory floor, but not all of it. If she kept close to the wall, she could move through a region of deep shadow, then dash the final few feet. She had to try.

She took a breath, counted to three, and *ran*.

She very nearly made it to the door. But then a hand grabbed her collar from behind, choking her with a sound of tearing fabric. Dimmock wrenched her around to face him. He held her by the shoulders and shook her.

'What the devil are you about, eh?'

Jostled and shaken, Lizzie couldn't even speak.

Dimmock flung her to the ground. Jolts of pain shot up from her knee and elbow where she landed.

'I knew you'd be trouble,' he leered. 'From the second I laid eyes on you. We've had your sort in here before. Think hard work's beneath them.' He took a short leather whip, like a riding crop, from his belt. Lizzie's eyes widened as she saw it. 'You just need to be broken in. Like a bad dog.' He advanced on her, whip raised and ready to strike.

Lizzie sprang to her feet and balled her fists. 'Get *away* from me!'

Dimmock stopped in his tracks and a look of momentary confusion passed over his face. Lizzie guessed nobody had tried to fight back before – all around, workers were staring at them.

Then Dimmock went on the attack. The whip lashed out. Lizzie darted to one side. The whip struck the wall with a sound like cracking bones. He grunted, slashing again. 'Hold still, ye wee she dev—'

Lizzie snatched up the pitcher of milk from the lunch trolley and flung it at him.

Drenched, Dimmock staggered backwards, spluttering and howling, while Lizzie stood amazed at what she had done. A girl gasped.

Right then, the door to the office flung open from inside and Alexander MacDonald stood there glaring. 'What's all this commotion about?'

'I'm blinded!' Dimmock howled. 'Call the police!'

'Lizzie?' MacDonald stared at Lizzie in complete confusion. 'What are you ... ? Never mind. Get in here!'

'She's an animal!'

'That will do, Mr Dimmock,' MacDonald said firmly. 'Put Deakin in charge, and take ten minutes to calm yourself.' With that, he grabbed Lizzie by the wrist and pulled her into his office.

The door shut behind her with a slam and Lizzie glanced around the luxurious room. The carpet was wine-red, the desk as dark and shiny as a coffin. Tall portraits loomed down from the oak-panelled walls. Had she seen this room before, in one of her visions? She couldn't even remember. Her day of mind-numbing work, coming on the heels of a sleepless night, had left her dizzy and slightly hysterical.

She could see the safe in the wall was open, and piles of money lay on the desk. It confirmed everything suspected. *Yes*, she thought. *He's doing it for the money. If he's killed Amelia, then the whole mill is his.*

She rounded on him. 'I know Amelia's here!' she yelled. 'Where is she?'

For the second time, MacDonald stared at her, completely perplexed. 'What?'

'Have you done it yet?' Her voice shook. She was crying, she realized, but it didn't seem to matter. Nothing mattered any more except Amelia.

'Done what, you preposterous girl?'

'Have you killed her?' Lizzie asked in a half-scream. 'Please don't. Please tell me she's not dead!'

MacDonald retreated behind his desk, poured himself a whisky and downed it in one. 'You aren't making any sense,' he said wearily. 'Let me make a deal with you. Calm down, stop screaming, and I will tell you what this money is for. Then you can tell me why you are here in my mill, causing trouble. Agreed?'

'All right,' Lizzie said. The room felt like it was spinning. She sat down heavily in a velvet-lined chair.

'I'm emptying out the safe to pay Douglas Grant his fee,' MacDonald said. 'All this money – it's meaningless compared to finding her alive.'

Lizzie's mouth fell open. 'He's asking that much?'

'Yes.'

'In return for finding Amelia?'

'Yes. So far he has told me nothing. Except to accuse you, of course. And yet, here you are…' His voice trailed off. On the wall hung a photograph of Amelia, smiling, in an oval frame. MacDonald propped himself against the wall with one hand and stared at it. Tears filled his eyes. Suddenly he lifted it off the wall and hugged it to himself, sobbing and rocking back and forth. 'I love her so much,' he whispered through his tears. 'More than anything in this whole rotten world.'

Lizzie stood up. Seeing MacDonald like this had brought her to her senses again. 'Grant is just using you, sir,' she told him. 'He cannot help you. But I believe I can.' Very gently she put her hands on the photograph. 'May I?'

MacDonald hesitated, reluctant to let go, and then nodded.

Lizzie turned the photograph around. She looked into the little girl's smiling face – and the link was suddenly *there*, sure and clear, like a memory jolted back into life. For some reason, the photograph captured more of her essence than a whole room of her possessions. A vision formed in her mind, so intense it made her head hurt.

She was looking through Amelia's eyes. From the shape of the windows she could see and the background noises she could hear, Lizzie knew the girl was inside the mill.

Amelia opened her mouth to speak, but a hand came down to cover it up. A voice said, 'Shh, Amelia, you don't want your uncle to find you, do you?'

Even before the voice spoke a word, Lizzie realized who it was.

The hand was missing a finger.

'It's Maisie,' she said.

'Her nursemaid?'

'Yes! Maisie's got her. And she's here, inside the mill!'

MacDonald's eyes blazed with anger. 'Come with me!'

Factory workers stepped aside, staring in silent amazement, as Lizzie and MacDonald burst out of the office and ran past them together. 'Up the stairs!' he shouted. 'Amelia, come out!'

'Amelia!' Lizzie yelled. 'It's all right, we're coming!'

They stampeded up the stairs to the next floor, where a sea of looms was whirring and clacking. MacDonald ran ahead, still shouting his niece's name. Lizzie wove back and forth, looking to the left and right, straining for any sign of Maisie or the girl.

She tried to match the factory floor she saw with what she'd seen in her vision, but the windows all looked the same, and the vision had been over so quickly. Swearing to herself, she ran between two looms, almost falling over a scruffy little boy who darted out in front of her.

'Move!' she yelled at him.

The boy grabbed at her sleeve and Lizzie stepped back and looked at him – his big blue eyes, his shaved head – and wondered where she might have seen him before. For a moment, she had the mad thought that he could be a changeling. Despite his grubby clothes, the little boy had the other-worldly look of a fairy child about him.

'Lizzie!' the child said excitedly.

It couldn't be. Lizzie stared down at the child's stubbly head. The tiny hairs were golden. In that moment, she *knew*. Someone had done their best to disguise the child, dressing her up in shabby boys' clothes, shaving her head and smearing her face with dirt, but this was no little boy.

'*Amelia?*'

'Don't tell Uncle Ally I'm here!' Amelia whispered, putting her finger to her lips. 'I'm playing hide and seek.'

Lizzie let out a sob of relief and joy. 'Oh no you're not, my darling. You're coming home.'

She reached out with both arms and stepped forward to gather Amelia up.

Next moment, a hand with one missing finger

descended onto Amelia's shoulder and pulled her back, roughly. A harsh voice rang out.

'Not another step, Lizzie Brown, or I'll throw her in the machine!'

CHAPTER 16

Maisie had changed since Lizzie had seen her last, just a few days before. Her eyes were wild, her hair in disarray. She held onto Amelia like a prize.

Would she really throw Amelia into the machine? Lizzie prayed not – but there was no telling what this woman was capable of.

'It was you all along,' Lizzie said. 'Why? Why would you want to hurt an innocent little girl?'

'I've not hurt her,' Maisie said. 'God willing, I won't have to.'

'Then why take her?'

'Because of *him*!' Maisie pointed angrily at Alexander

MacDonald. He had caught sight of them and was sprinting back down the hall towards them.

'Stay back!' ordered Maisie.

'Best do as she says,' Lizzie warned.

MacDonald staggered to a halt, only yards away from Maisie. Amelia jerked towards him, but Maisie's iron fingers gripped her so tightly she moaned with pain.

'*Now* you see her, eh, MacDonald?' Maisie said bitterly. 'You've walked past her a dozen times and never spared her a glance. Just another mill brat like all the others. But now you see she's your own flesh and blood, suddenly you care!'

MacDonald spoke very slowly and carefully. 'Maisie, in the name of mercy, let her go. She's only a child. Please, I beg you!'

'Mercy!' Maisie let out a wild laugh. 'When I came to work in your mill at the age of eight, did you show me mercy then?' She brandished her mutilated finger. 'I slaved on your machines, day after dreary day! No mercy, even when the spinning mule tore my finger off!' She glared at Lizzie. 'They docked my pay, you know. I bled on the cloth. A whole bolt was ruined.'

'Maisie,' Lizzie begged, 'you can't make Amelia

suffer just because you did.'

'Did? *Did?* I'm still here! Oh, I thought I'd left this rotten place behind me, the day I finally scraped together enough money to move on. I found a position I could be proud of. Nursemaid in service to Alexander MacDonald himself! Until he threw me out. You saw. You were there.'

'There was nowhere else you could go … ?' Lizzie said. 'So you came back here.' She felt genuinely sorry for Maisie, but the woman stared at her with a face full of hate, as if Lizzie's pity made her sick.

'Aye, I came back. Where else could I do honest work without a reference? I hoped things might have changed for the better, but of course they hadn't. *His* sort only care about money. They don't give a damn for the people who toil here, no better than slaves! So I had to make him care. I had to make him *see*!'

Lizzie looked from Maisie to Amelia and back. 'So that's why you took Amelia. To show MacDonald how bad this place really was.'

Maisie gave a triumphant nod. 'The likes of me don't matter to him. He'd never improve conditions just for our sake. But if it were someone he loved…'

'I'm sorry I fired you.' MacDonald fell to his knees.

'Let her go, and I'll give you anything you want.'

'Ha!'

'Your old job back. All the money in my safe … even more!'

Maisie laughed. 'You're a blind old fool! This isn't about the *money*. It's about *change*. Nobody should have to work in conditions like these. Especially not little children!'

MacDonald looked around at the silent workers. 'Very well. I'll make reforms. I swear it before all of you.' He held out his hand. 'You can let her go now.'

A long moment passed and Lizzie held her breath, waiting for Amelia to go running into her uncle's arms.

But Maisie shook her head sadly and gripped the little girl all the tighter. 'Ach, you'd swear that black is white if it got you your niece back. I'm no' stupid, sir. I know I'll be bundled off to the police the second I let Amelia go.'

Amelia looked at her uncle now, wide-eyed. 'Don't be angry with Maisie, Uncle Ally. We were only playing hide and seek. And it was such a good hiding place, wasn't it? It took you *days* to find me!'

Maisie pulled Amelia into a firm embrace. 'That's right, my elf.' She kissed the top of the girl's head. 'You were very brave. We were going to send your Uncle Ally a letter, saying that you would come back if he made the mill better for its workers. But then Lizzie Brown had to go and ruin it all.'

'I was trying to *save* her!' Lizzie yelled.

'*Save* her? You've *doomed* her.' Maisie shook her head and began to cry, great hitching sobs of total despair. 'Everything's ruined. I'll never leave this place alive. Somehow I always knew I'd die here…'

Lizzie made up her mind to rush her. The woman was half-mad with grief and rage, so if she was quick, she could grab Amelia and pull her out of Maisie's reach.

Too late. Maisie started pulling Amelia towards the stairwell.

Alexander MacDonald bellowed, 'Men! Get her! Ten guineas for the man who does!'

A group of burly mill workers immediately ran towards Maisie. Howling, she dragged Amelia up the stairs to an upper landing. As the men closed in on her, she backed into a pedestal where one of the tall whale-oil lamps stood.

'Get back!' she screeched. 'Traitors. Rogues!'

One of the men lunged for her and Maisie fell

back, knocking the pedestal over. The lamp fell with a crash, rolling down the stairs and leaking burning oil as it went. With cries of alarm, the men all fled from its path.

'Oh God,' Lizzie gasped as it tumbled past. 'Someone fetch a bucket of water, *now*!'

But it was already too late for that. The shattered remains of the lamp came to rest at the bottom of the stairs, but the burning oil spread out like a carpet.

The bare wooden floorboards blackened and charred. Flames licked up the side of a stack of rolled cloth, and it caught fire instantly. It might as well have been a stacked bonfire ready for Guy Fawkes Night, Lizzie saw with horror. This place was a tinderbox just waiting to go up.

By the time the first buckets of water arrived, the fire was already burning out of control. A whole corner of the factory floor was alight and workers had already begun to make their way towards the exits, abandoning their machines to their fate.

Lizzie started towards the stairs where Maisie and Amelia had gone. A thick curtain of smoke hid them from sight. She backed off, coughing.

'Damp down the cloth!' MacDonald yelled.

'Dimmock, shut the machines down, for God's sake!'

But within minutes, the whole main factory floor was dense with black smoke and leaping flames. The glowing tongues licked at the support beams in the ceiling.

MacDonald and Lizzie joined a bucket chain. They flung water into the inferno, but it was clear the fire had taken hold and couldn't be quenched. The machines were burning now. Yarn sizzled and glowed like the fuses on dynamite sticks. A metallic groan and crash announced a boiler had collapsed.

Lizzie coughed and wiped her streaming eyes. 'You've got to get your people out of here!'

'I'm not going anywhere without Amelia!'

'I'll get her,' Lizzie said. 'You get everyone else out.'

'But she's my niece!'

'*Think!* Maisie doesn't hate me like she hates you!' Lizzie yelled. 'We've got things in common – she might listen to me!'

MacDonald nodded. 'You're right. God go with you, Miss Brown. Everybody out!'

The cry went up from person to person throughout the building: 'Everybody out!' A stampede of workers and supervisors began as people grappled their way to the exits. Someone flung a stool through a window, shattering it, and workers on the upper floors came charging down the stairs, holding wet cloth over their mouths and noses, coughing hard.

Lizzie looked back up the stairs. That was where she had to go. The factory might be burning down, but Amelia was still up there...

CHAPTER 17

Lizzie pushed her way through the stampede of terrified workers. 'You want to go *down*, girl!' one of them shouted. 'The mill's on fire!'

'I know!' she grunted, shoving past him. 'Let me through.'

Harsh, acrid smoke made her cough. Her head spun. Half-starved and exhausted, she struggled through the crowd step by step.

'Amelia!' she shouted, her throat hoarse. 'Where are you?'

She broke through the last of the mill workers, charged around the landing and sprinted up to the very top floor.

She was in a long hallway, right under the roof. The sloping sides gave the whole room a triangular shape while at the end, a round window showed a gloomy sky. Only a few whale-oil lamps lit the place.

Down both sides of the room, to the left and right, stacks of cloth had been piled up. It was like an immense loft. This must be a fabric storehouse – and when the fire reached it, it would burn like dry grass. Smoke was already curling up from the gaps between the floorboards.

Somewhere, among these musty heaps of fabric reaching up to the diagonal ceiling, Maisie and Amelia must be hiding. There was no other way out of the place.

From downstairs Lizzie heard shouts and screams, then a terrific crash, and the floor vibrated below her feet. One of the machines must have collapsed.

'Maisie?' she called nervously. 'Amelia? You've got to get out!'

Maisie shuffled out from behind one of the end stacks, still holding Amelia to her like a life-size doll. She stood in front of the window and stared at Lizzie with white, wild eyes.

'Can't you smell the smoke?' Lizzie pleaded.

Maisie took a deep sniff and laughed bitterly. 'This place, it's tasted Hendry blood before. My sister died here, you see.'

'How?' Lizzie tried to ask, and burst out coughing.

'Like that,' Maisie said, with an insane chuckle. 'Fibres in the air. It gets into your lungs and you rot away from the inside.' She sniffed. 'Jinnie died at her machine, coughing up blood. They dragged her away and someone took her place like they always do. But not any more. I'll die here. I know that. But I'll be the last.'

Lizzie slowly moved towards her, holding her hands out. 'I can't imagine what you've been through,' she said. 'To drive you to this … they were cruel to you. Wicked. It's unforgivable.'

'You sound like her uncle. You were here for *one day*!' Maisie yelled. 'What can you know?'

'I know *enough*! My brother died in a factory!' Lizzie screamed back at her. 'An' I loved him, just like you loved your sister, so don't you *dare* tell me I'm like MacDonald!'

Maisie stood trembling, then gave Lizzie a sad, almost sisterly smile. Lizzie crept even closer, praying she could get near enough. She was almost at the window now. She passed by a pile of spare machine parts: wooden shuttles, gears, odd twists of metal she didn't recognize.

'It can't go on, can it?' Maisie said, tears flowing down her face. 'The owners must change their ways.'

'They have to.'

'No more of this slavery. Or there'll be a reckoning. A red dawn.'

'Maisie,' Lizzie pleaded, 'you've done what you meant to do. MacDonald's scared half to death. So just let Amelia go.' Desperately she tried to think of the right thing to say. 'She's only a child. You aren't going to make a child suffer like MacDonald does, are you?'

Maisie wept and clung onto Amelia, rocking her back and forth.

'Maisie, for the love of God! If we don't leave now, we'll all be killed!'

'Can't stop now,' Maisie sobbed. 'Come too far to turn back. We'll all go together, won't we? Off to Fairyland in the dancing flames.' She smiled down at Amelia, who stared back at her in silent terror. 'And your uncle won't ever forget us. We'll be dead, but all the boys and girls that come after will be safe.

Because he'll have learned his lesson.'

Lizzie knew then that Maisie was determined to die. Nothing she could say would change that. Thinking quickly, she grabbed one of the loose shuttles and flung it at Maisie. It struck her in the head with a grisly crack and Maisie let go of Amelia and sank to her knees, groaning and clutching her head.

Lizzie grabbed Amelia, hugged the little girl to her, then glanced back at the stairwell. To her dismay she saw greedy flames were already leaping up inside it like an oven.

Amelia coughed and gasped. 'Lizzie, I'm scared.'

'So am I.'

The smoke was growing thicker. Lizzie wrenched at the window fastening, but it was rusted shut. She sagged in hopeless defeat, then felt Amelia gently hug her again. Big eyes gazed up into hers, full of trust.

No. I'm not giving up!

With her elbow she bashed and bashed at the handle. Flakes of rust flew, and her arm burned with pain – then suddenly the window came free, half a circle of glass creaking open. Cold, sweet, fresh air rushed into the room.

Lizzie gasped, her throat aching. She looked down,

and her stomach lurched. The factory wall fell away like a brick chimney, the cobbled yard spreading out impossibly far below. There was no ladder.

'There they are!' shouted MacDonald from the yard. A crowd of people stood with him, their faces turned up, full of pity and horror.

Lizzie gripped the window frame, paralysed by panic. Soon, the flames would reach the room, or the floor would collapse from under them. If they jumped, they would fall to their deaths.

No safety net here. Desperate, she looked around for salvation. Her gaze fell on a stack of rolled-up bolts of fabric, and an idea took hold of her mind.

She grabbed one of the rolls and heaved for all she was worth. Somehow she managed to drag it to the window. She changed ends and shoved it until the whole thing was hanging out, then kicked it until it fell down, unravelling like a flag on the way.

'Stretch it out!' she yelled. 'Like a safety net!'

MacDonald understood. The crowd took hold of the edges of the cloth and pulled.

A roaring, crashing sound made Lizzie look back into the factory. The floor was falling in, piece by piece. A crimson glow flickered across Amelia's face.

Lizzie grabbed her. 'We've got to jump.'

'Nooo!' Amelia kicked and tried to pull away. 'I can't!'

'Yes. You can. It's time to fly, Amelia. Like a fairy! Then you can bounce, just like at the circus.'

'Bouncing?'

'The biggest bounce you ever did.' The floor beneath Lizzie's feet groaned. Hot light shone between the cracks. 'Hurry!' She quickly kissed the little girl on her forehead.

Obediently Amelia sat on the window ledge. 'I'm going to fly,' she whispered. 'One, two, three ... *wheee!*' She jumped – and vanished from sight.

From the yard below came a rising chorus of screams. Lizzie couldn't bear to look.

Deep in the factory, something exploded with a bang and a rattle. The heat was unbearable now. She ran over to Maisie, grabbed her by the arm and dragged her over to the window.

'No!' wailed Maisie, trying to fight Lizzie off. 'Leave me alone. I'll die here in this factory – just as I always knew I would.'

'Not if I can help it,' Lizzie said grimly. Yanking with all her might, she pulled the wounded woman to the window, then pushed her out. Screams came from below as Maisie fell towards the cloth safety net.

Lizzie gazed wildly around the factory floor, checking that nobody was left. With a loud groan, the floor sagged and began to collapse. As quickly as she could, she lifted herself onto the window ledge.

She closed her eyes, crossed her fingers – and jumped.

CHAPTER 18

Lizzie dreamed of falling. From high in the clouds she fell, down and down, until she woke with a jolt.

Stiff white sheets, stretched tightly over her. A strange chemical smell, mingled with the scent of flowers. This wasn't her bed. She was in a hospital, with a room to herself.

She sat up and winced. Her left leg stung, and so did her right shoulder – but someone had bandaged them. She touched the shoulder experimentally and hissed through her teeth. A burn. Funny, she didn't remember being burned.

Her chest hurt. When she coughed, she tasted

smoke. Images began to come back to her – the burning mill, the screams, the flames leaping through the floorboards.

I'm alive, she thought. *I made it*. She reached for the mug of water by the bed and noticed an immense bunch of flowers in a vase. Who on earth had sent her flowers? And why wasn't she out on the ward with all the other patients?

A nurse noticed she was awake and bustled over, smiling. 'Morning!'

'Is it?' Lizzie brushed tousled hair out of her face.

'Only just,' the nurse laughed. 'It's almost noon.'

Lizzie tried to struggle out of bed. 'There must be some mistake,' she said. 'I can't afford this room—'

The nurse smiled and gently pushed her back into the bed. 'Mr MacDonald wants you to have the best possible treatment, Lizzie. He's paying for your care,' she explained. 'Now then, do you feel up to seeing visitors?'

Before Lizzie could answer, the door burst open and Nora ran to her bedside, with Erin, Malachy, Dru and Hari close behind. They surrounded her bed, hugging her, laughing and piling wrapped presents onto the cabinets.

'Steady on!' Lizzie protested. 'Don't break me!'

'Sorry,' grinned Nora. 'But we're so glad you're all right!'

'If you were a cat, you'd be on your last life by now,' Erin added.

Lizzie grabbed Malachy's wrist, suddenly remembering. 'Is Amelia … ?'

'She's fine!' he said. His eyes widened in surprise. 'Wait, don't you remember what happened?'

Lizzie settled back on her pillows, finally feeling like she could rest. 'I remember jumping,' she said. 'But after that it's a blank. You'll have to fill me in.'

Everyone sat down on the bed while Nora softly explained. 'The mill burned down. Just after you jumped, it all fell in, like a house of cards. They caught you on that cloth, but you were out cold.'

'Did I hit my head?'

'The doctors think you passed out on the way down! You were in a shocking state, Liz. Half-dead from the smoke.'

Half-dead, Lizzie thought. 'Did anybody die?'

Nora put a hand on Lizzie's arm. 'A few. Three of them were workers who went back in to try to pull others out. It's a mercy more weren't killed.'

'And Maisie?'

Her friends exchanged looks.

'She was one of the ones who died,' said Erin. 'She survived the fall, but her lungs had inhaled too much smoke.'

Lizzie closed her eyes and thought about Maisie's last words. *She knew she was going to die there. Maybe she had a touch of the second sight too.*

'Well,' she said, trying to lighten the mood, 'at least we know it wasn't the fairies who took Amelia.'

'Now it's funny you should say that,' Hari piped up. 'We've solved a mystery of our own, and we didn't even need your visions for help!'

Malachy laughed. 'Of course. Remember how Ma Sullivan's cakes were stolen and your crystal ball went missing? Not to mention all the other funny little happenings?'

'Course I do. Ma Sullivan blamed it on the fairies.'

'It was Hanu the monkey!' Hari said. 'His fingers are even more nimble than I thought. He worked out how to open his cage door.'

'We only put two and two together when we found your crystal ball in his cage with him,' chuckled Malachy. 'So that wasn't fairies either.'

Nora and Erin glowered at him. 'You needn't be so smug,' Nora said. 'Just because it was a monkey *this* time, it doesn't prove that fairies don't exist.'

'You're right,' Lizzie smiled. 'It doesn't.'

Taken completely by surprise, Nora boggled at her.

Lizzie winked. 'If working at Fitzy's has taught me anything, it's to keep an open mind.'

'Ready for another visitor?' The nurse showed Fergus into the room.

'Now I know you're through with newspapers, but I thought you might like to have a look at this one,' he said.

The front page screamed: CIRCUS GIRL SAVES MILL HEIRESS. Under that, in smaller writing: DID KINDLY SPIRITS HELP FOIL CAPTOR'S PLOT?

Malachy was all for reading the story, but Lizzie stopped him. 'Amelia's safe and I'm back in MacDonald's good books,' she said. 'That'll do for me.'

'Sounds like he wants to be in *your* good books,' Fergus said. He pointed out another feature: MILL TYCOON JOINS REFORMISTS.

'*The industrialist Alexander MacDonald has pledged to rebuild his mill to the highest safety standards,*' Malachy read aloud. '*In addition, he has announced his plans to campaign Parliament to pass new labour laws prohibiting the employment of children under the age of ten in factories. "It is my wish to set an example to the whole textile industry," MacDonald says. "My eyes have been opened to a great wrong."'*

'Better late than never,' Lizzie murmured. *Now maybe Maisie can rest in peace, poor troubled soul.*

'Oh, and what's this little bit on the back?' Malachy laughed, showing Lizzie a picture of Douglas Grant. The headline read: DISGRACED PSYCHIC RETURNS TO AMERICA.

'He's been exorcized, like a troublesome spirit,' said Nora.

'Good riddance!' said Lizzie, and broke into a fresh bout of coughing.

'I think visiting time's over,' the nurse said, gentle but firm. 'Lizzie needs to rest. You can come back tomorrow.'

Hugs and kisses followed. Left alone in her room, Lizzie closed her eyes. *My friends are wonderful*, she thought. *More wonderful than fairies could ever be.*

* * *

'Good to see you back on your feet, Lizzie!' Fergus grinned, a few days later. He was leaning against the front gates of Alexander MacDonald's house. In the courtyard, the members of Fitzy's Travelling Circus busied themselves with preparations. The temporary stage was nearly complete and the air crackled with excitement.

Lizzie let him in. 'Does MacDonald know you're here?'

'He invited me,' Fergus said, beaming with pride. 'I'm covering the story for the paper as their newly appointed *Chief* Reporter.'

'It's Amelia's welcome home party, not a bloomin' royal gala!' Lizzie laughed. 'But congratulations on the promotion, mate.' They strolled over to where the house door stood propped open. 'I told you you'd be a success, didn't I?'

'You did. But keep quiet about the thumb, eh?'

MacDonald and Amelia were waiting in the parlour, along with someone else sitting in a chair with its back to them. Amelia had a beautiful silk party dress on, a pretty ribbon around her shorn head, and a pair of gauzy fairy wings on her back. Her uncle – to Lizzie's delight – was wearing pointy ears made out of wax.

'How's the guest of honour?' he called to her. 'Ah, Fergus, you made it. Welcome.'

The unseen figure in the chair stood up and Lizzie heard Fergus catch his breath.

It was Collette, barely recognizable in her smart, formal clothes. Her hair had been put up and she stood demurely with her hands clasped behind her back.

'Of course,' MacDonald said, 'you haven't heard, have you, Fergus? Mademoiselle Boisset has done me the great honour of joining our household.'

Fergus's jaw worked and he loosened his collar. He seemed at a loss for what to say. 'C-congratulations to you both,' he said nobly. 'I wish you many happy years together.'

Collette stared and burst out laughing. 'We're not married, you great *imbecile!* I'm Amelia's governess. And French tutor.'

'Oh!' said Fergus. He sank into a chair, laughing in relief. 'Well, that's splendid.'

'I know French now!' Amelia yelled. '*Bonjour! Je voudrais un biscuit! Merci, Mademoiselle Lizzie!*'

Collette rolled her eyes. 'All day, she says this. "*Merci, Mademoiselle Lizzie.*" Like a little bird.'

'But she did save me, Mademoiselle Collette.'

'That she did,' Collette smiled, squeezing the little girl's hand.

MacDonald went off to supervise the preparations and Lizzie decided to satisfy her curiosity about something. 'Amelia,' she asked quietly, 'do you remember what happened in the woods that day?'

'I ran off to the oak tree to hide and Maisie was there – just like she said she would be. All dressed in fairy clothes! I thought we were going to have a fairy tea party, like we usually did, but Maisie said no, we were still going to play hide and seek. Only she knew the best hiding place ever, ever, ever.'

'The mill,' Lizzie sighed.

'I *was* a bit scared,' Amelia admitted. 'But it was so lovely to see Maisie again! She told me stories and sang me my favourite songs again. She said we were just playing a game.' She frowned deeply, as if she was trying to be very grown-up. 'Lizzie?'

'Yes?'

'Was Maisie … bad?'

Lizzie said carefully 'No. She was a person that bad things happened to. People were cruel to her for years, and it hurt her in her mind, so she didn't know right from wrong any more. I'm sure she never meant to do you any harm.'

Amelia took that in. 'The mill was horrible,' she said. 'But Uncle Ally says the new mill will be nice, and he'll pay the workers more money so they won't be sad any more.' She sprang to her feet. 'Look, Lizzie, clowns! I'm going to play with them!'

'You do that.'

Lizzie joined Collette on the sofa and relaxed, letting out a deep sigh. 'I still can't believe you're leaving us. Do you think you'll miss it?' Alexander MacDonald had offered Collette her new job while Lizzie had been in the hospital, and it still hadn't really sunk in.

'Of course I shall,' Collette said. 'But the circus comes to Edinburgh once a year so I will see everyone then. I'm ready to settle down. No more high wire. No more backaches.'

'Lucky Amelia. You'll make a brilliant mum one day.'

Collette giggled and looked away shyly. 'Maybe Amelia can be my bridesmaid, when I find a husband.'

Across the room, Fergus turned an impressive shade of red. *I knew it*, Lizzie thought. *Amelia isn't the only reason Collette wants to stay in Edinburgh!*

'Show starts in half an hour!' Fitzy announced,

striding into the room. 'How are you feeling, Lizzie? Full of zest? Full of zing? Ready to go back to work?'

'Can't wait!'

'That's my girl.'

'So after today, where are we heading next?'

'Well, *we're* heading south to Manchester,' Fitzy said. 'Those that aren't staying here, that is.' He winked at Collette. 'Which brings me to something else. Lizzie … you mustn't feel you have to come with us.'

Lizzie cocked her head. 'Come again?'

'You're famous!' Fitzy burst out. 'Your star has never risen higher. You could go anywhere in the country – anywhere in the *world* – and be welcomed with open arms! I can't expect you to trek about with my circus for the rest of your life, can I?'

Lizzie smiled. 'Right now, there's nowhere I'd rather be.'

Don't miss the first book in

THE
MAGNIFICENT LIZZIE BROWN
series

Roll up, roll up! A hair-raising adventure is about to unfold!

Join Lizzie Brown, the fortuneteller's assistant, and her gang of circus friends, as they try to uncover the identity of the mysterious phantom.

In Victorian London, a masked figure has been thieving from houses and evading the police. When Lizzie Brown has a psychic vision about the burglar, she knows she has to act. But this phantom is proving to be more dangerous than a tightrope without a safety net…

Don't miss the second book in

THE
MAGNIFICENT LIZZIE BROWN
series

Something terrifying is circling the circus's new pitch.
The locals speak of a monster known to roam the nearby
cemetery. But Lizzie Brown doesn't believe it.

After a chilling message from beyond the grave and a
meeting with some mysterious criminals, Lizzie and her
gang confront the so-called 'devil's hound'. But they find
the story has only just begun…

Don't miss the third book in

THE
MAGNIFICENT LIZZIE BROWN
series

Lizzie and the circus are in Whitby, a town that doesn't
seem to want them there. The only friendly faces are the
glamorous Maharajah and his beautiful but secretive wife.

So when Lizzie and her gang spot a glowing galleon off the
coast, why are all clues pointing towards the town's most
eye-catching couple?

For more exciting books from brilliant
authors, follow the fox!
www.curious-fox.com

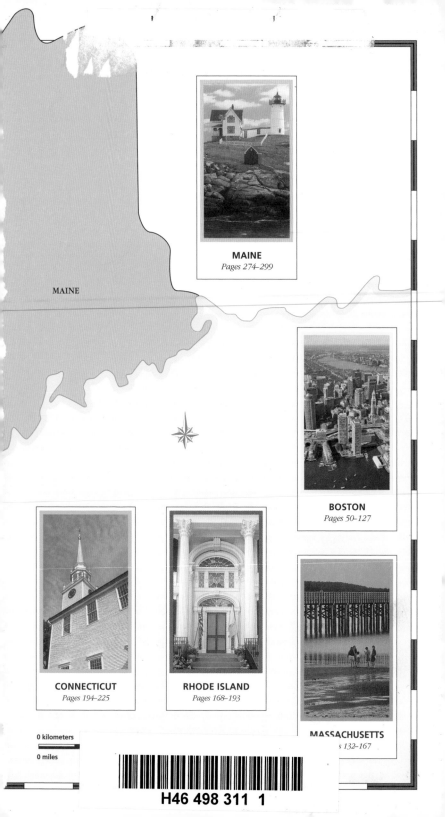

MAINE

MAINE
Pages 274–299

BOSTON
Pages 50–127

CONNECTICUT
Pages 194–225

RHODE ISLAND
Pages 168–193

MASSACHUSETTS
Pages 132–167

0 kilometers

0 miles

H46 498 311 1